END OF THE TRAIL

Desperately Fargo tried the ropes that bound him. They held fast. He worked his mouth to rid himself of his gag. No use. Fraco had done a good job on him. That was to be expected. Fraco liked to do his work well. He had gone to get tongs that would turn red-hot to make sure Fargo died in slow agony.

Fargo heard footsteps. The sound of death.

But it wasn't Fraco. The tall gunman in black stood in front of the Trailsman. He was the man who'd been trailing Fargo for so long.

"I finally caught up with you," he said.

Fargo tried to speak, but the gag muffled his words. There would be no pleading for mercy with this killer. And no bargaining.

The man's black eyes glittered above his broken nose. His silver pistol glinted in his hand. He aimed it straight at Fargo. As his gunshot exploded, Fargo's last thought was that at least this way he would die fast. . . .

**BE SURE TO READ THE
OTHER BOOKS IN THIS EXCITING
TRAILSMAN SERIES!**

COYOTE RUN
BY DON BENDELL

On one side stood the legendary Chief of Scouts, Chris Colt, with his hair-trigger tempered, half brother Joshua, and the proud young Indian brave, Man Killer. On the other side was a mining company that would do anything and kill anyone to take over Coyote Run, the ranch that the Colts had carved out of the Sangre Cristo Mountains, with their sweat and their blood. Their battle would flame amid the thunder of a cattle drive, the tumult of a dramatic courtroom trial, the howling of a lynch mob, and a struggle for an entire town. And as the savagery mounted, the stakes rose higher and higher, and every weapon from gun and knife to a brave lawyer's eloquent tongue and the strength and spirit of two beautiful women came into powerful play.

from SIGNET

Buy them at your local bookstore or use this convenient coupon for ordering.

PENGUIN USA
P.O. Box 999 — Dept. #17109
Bergenfield, New Jersey 07621

Please send me the books I have checked above.
I am enclosing $_____ (please add $2.00 to cover postage and handling). Send check or money order (no cash or C.O.D.'s) or charge by Mastercard or VISA (with a $15.00 minimum). Prices and numbers are subject to change without notice.

Card #_____ Exp. Date _____
Signature_____
Name_____
Address_____
City _____ State _____ Zip Code _____

For faster service when ordering by credit card call **1-800-253-6476**

Allow a minimum of 4-6 weeks for delivery. This offer is subject to change without notice.

BLACK MESA TREACHERY

by

Jon Sharpe

A SIGNET BOOK

SIGNET
Published by the Penguin Group
Penguin Books USA Inc., 375 Hudson Street,
New York, New York 10014, U.S.A.
Penguin Books Ltd, 27 Wrights Lane,
London W8 5TZ, England
Penguin Books Australia Ltd, Ringwood,
Victoria, Australia
Penguin Books Canada Ltd, 10 Alcorn Avenue,
Toronto, Ontario, Canada M4V 3B2
Penguin Books (N.Z.) Ltd, 182–190 Wairau Road,
Auckland 10, New Zealand

Penguin Books Ltd, Registered Offices:
Harmondsworth, Middlesex, England

First published by Signet, an imprint of Dutton Signet,
a division of Penguin Books USA Inc.

First Printing, November, 1995
10 9 8 7 6 5 4 3 2 1

Copyright © Jon Sharpe, 1995
All rights reserved

The first chapter of this book previously appeared in *Colorado Carnage*,
the one hundred sixty-sixth volume in this series.

 REGISTERED TRADEMARK—MARCA REGISTRADA

Printed in the United States of America

Without limiting the rights under copyright reserved above, no part of
this publication may be reproduced, stored in or introduced into a
retrieval system, or transmitted, in any form, or by any means (electronic,
mechanical, photocopying, recording, or otherwise), without the prior
written permission of both the copyright owner and the above publisher
of this book.

BOOKS ARE AVAILABLE AT QUANTITY DISCOUNTS WHEN USED TO PROMOTE
PRODUCTS OR SERVICES. FOR INFORMATION PLEASE WRITE TO PREMIUM
MARKETING DIVISION, PENGUIN BOOKS USA INC., 375 HUDSON STREET, NEW
YORK, NEW YORK 10014.

If you purchased this book without a cover you should be aware that this
book is stolen property. It was reported as "unsold and destroyed" to the
publisher and neither the author nor the publisher has received any
payment for this "stripped book."

The Trailsman

Beginnings . . . they bend the tree and they mark the man. Skye Fargo was born when he was eighteen. Terror was his midwife, vengeance his first cry. Killing spawned Skye Fargo, ruthless, cold-blooded murder. Out of the acrid smoke of gunpowder still hanging in the air, he rose, cried out a promise never forgotten.

The Trailsman they began to call him all across the West: searcher, scout, hunter, the man who could see where others only looked, his skills for hire but not his soul, the man who lived each day to the fullest, yet trailed each tomorrow. Skye Fargo, the Trailsman, and the seeker who could take the wildness of a land and the wanting of a woman and make them his own.

*The high plateau near Santa Fe, 1860—
a harsh land of red rock and rolling thunder,
where some men find the face of God
and others do the Devil's work . . .*

1

"You Skye Fargo?"

The tall man with the lake blue eyes glanced up from his whiskey at the rotund bartender who had spoken. Another man standing nearby, foot hooked over the bar rail and beer in hand, nudged his companion and the two of them gawked at the tall stranger.

"Did you hear that? That's Skye Fargo," one of them whispered to the other. "They call him the Trailsman. I heard all about him."

"Yeah, me too," the other whispered back, awe in his voice. "Wonder what he's doing down here in Taos?"

Skye Fargo nodded once to the bartender, paying no attention to the two men.

"Forgot to tell you earlier when you came in, Mister Fargo. Got a message for you," the bartender said, handing him a folded paper.

Fargo took it and pushed his empty glass across the bar and shook his head, refusing a refill. He examined the writing on the small envelope—his name in bold black letters—and the large wax seal on the back with its crucifix, initialed A and F. Yeah, it was the message he'd been waiting for all afternoon. He glared at the bartender, suspecting him of holding the letter back in order to sell a few more drinks. As he broke the seal, Fargo gazed around the half-deserted bar. Late afternoon sun poured in past the bat-wing doors. In a dark corner four men were playing a dead earnest game of poker as they had been all afternoon. A dove in a faded green dress was talking to a heavyset fellow, a rancher by the looks of him. And then there were the two men—cowpoke types—standing next to him and staring at his every move. Fargo turned away from them and opened the paper.

> Meet him at Castle Rock on the Thunder Trail, edge of Tewa land. At moonrise. Bring him to Chimayò. Meanwhile, travel incognito—danger everywhere. Go with God. Amado Fernandez

Moonrise. That was around midnight. Fargo glanced at the golden light across the warped board floor. It was getting on sunset. He'd never make it in time. It was at least five or six hours of fast riding to the rendezvous point. Hastily, he pulled a couple of coins out of his pocket, threw them on the counter, and turned to go.

"Hey! Hey!" one of the cowpokes called after him as he headed toward the door. "Ain't you Skye Fargo? Ain't you the Trailsman?" The men at the poker table lowered their cards and craned their necks to stare at him. Then a couple of them pointed at him and muttered to one another. Fargo ignored them all and pushed through the doors. Great. Everybody in the Taos barroom had got a good look at him. And the message had said to travel incognito. Well, at least he'd be out of town in no time.

At the stable he asked for the Ovaro and the stable boy brought it out. The pinto's black-and-white coat gleamed magnificently in the slanting light. It nuzzled Fargo.

"Beautiful horse you got here, Mister Fargo," the boy said, stroking the pinto's neck, reluctant to let go of the reins. Fargo mounted. The pinto moved restlessly under him, eager to be away on the trail.

"You're awful popular, Mister Fargo," the boy said.

"What do you mean?"

"Those two guys looking for you," the kid said. "I told them you were over at the hotel. Didn't they find you?"

"Two guys? What did they look like?"

The boy screwed up his face, remembering.

"The first was one of them Catholic padres. Came in on a donkey around midday. Said he had some letter for you." Fargo nodded, saying nothing. Yes, the brother who had brought the message from Padre Amado Fernandez. "And then just a quarter hour ago. Big fellow. Tall and all dressed in black. Smart like. Riding a chestnut. I asked if he didn't want to stable her, but he said he was in a hurry to find you. Was in an awful bad mood."

Fargo sat for a moment, in thought. Who was the man in black who'd followed him to Taos? Sounded like trouble for sure. Meanwhile, the sun was dropping swiftly over the distant mountain, staining the clouds bloodred. There was no time to lose, no time to find out what trouble was after him now. He had a job to do, a promise to keep. Fargo pulled a coin out of his pocket and flipped it to the kid.

"Tell him you found out I was heading due north. Up to Ute Country."

"Sure. Sure, Mister Fargo."

Fargo headed out, riding through the back streets toward the head of the trail that led south out of Taos. But the question preyed on his mind. Who the hell was on his tail? He decided to have a quick look and turned back into the alley that led toward the main square. He dismounted and walked forward to stand at the corner of a storefront where he was out of sight but had a good view.

All around the square bars were just starting to heat up for the night. The strains of a honky-tonk piano floated on the air, and several knots of men came into sight, swaggering in different directions toward the various watering holes. A line of horses was hitched in front of the Taos Hotel. Among them stood a glistening black-pointed chestnut. As Fargo watched, a tall broad-shouldered man dressed all in black came out of the front door of the hotel. Even from a distance, Fargo's keen gaze could discern his broken nose and his glittering black eyes. Fargo searched his mind, but couldn't remember having seen the face before. The tall man paused for a moment, looked up and down the square, and then stepped down the stairs, heading for one of the bars. Just then, Fargo spotted the stable boy running up the dusty street in pursuit to tell the stranger that he had headed north. Fargo didn't wait, but turned back, mounted the pinto and galloped out of town.

Who the hell was the big man? He'd never seen him before, but he could have been sent by any one of a hundred men who had reason to hunt him down, thought Fargo. If the man lived hard and fast, he made a lot of friends and just about as many enemies. Anyway, the kid would throw the stranger off his scent. There was no time to deal with him now.

The pinto's powerful legs pounded the trail as they climbed the hill. Soon the town of Taos lay behind them, a clutter of board and adobe buildings at the foot of the high snowy peaks to the east. West of town the sage plain stretched for miles toward the mountains at the horizon. As he gained the crest of the hill and the flatland fell away below, Fargo spotted the dark jagged line of the gorge where the mighty Rio Grande cut deep into the earth.

But right now his business lay to the south, and as they came over the top of the hill, Taos and the gorge disappeared from view and Fargo's thoughts turned to what lay ahead. It had been a few weeks since the first message had come from Padre Amado Fernandez. Fargo had met the priest years before at a mission in California. Fernandez had struck him as one of the few holy men who seemed to have his feet on the ground. In his California parish the priest had built an orphanage and a hospital and then got the whole town reorganized after it had been burnt to the ground by a raging brush fire. He'd had one of the most successful missions in the whole country. Then the local archbishop transferred him down to the famous Chimayò Mission near Santa Fe. That had been five years ago, and Fargo hadn't heard a word about Amado Fernandez since.

Then, the week before, a letter found him up in Kansas. The padre wrote that he needed Fargo's help. The instructions were to go to Taos and wait at the bar for a message. Fargo wondered what kind of trouble the padre could have got himself into. The message had said meet "him." But who was he supposed to be meeting at Castle Rock? Well, he'd find out soon enough.

The sunset colors were fading in the west and ahead of him the first star appeared over the southern horizon which was sharp with buttes. The trail arched over the hills, curved through the dense and fragrant piñons, then descended toward the rocky, open land.

He rode hard toward the rendezvous point—Thunder Trail and Castle Rock near Black Mesa. Fargo knew the mesa, a mammoth hulk of rock and earth with sheer cliffs rising straight up from the flat land below. Black Mesa could be seen for hundreds of miles around. But no matter how sunny the day, Black Mesa always seemed to be in shadow and now, with the light fading steadily, it was a darker shadow in the shade of the mountains to the west. He headed toward the spot, the pinto galloping full out on the hard-packed trail. No time to lose. It was a good five hours' ride to Castle Rock. And by then the moon would be up. He was going to be late. Whoever he was supposed to be meeting there would just have to wait.

The moon was a bright silver coin high in the black heavens. Fargo stood and stretched his limbs, then leaned against the night-cold stone in the shadow of Castle Rock. All around him the nubby sage was like a woolen blanket folded over the moon-washed hills. A few miles away, the huge dark shape of Black Mesa blocked out the stars in the sky. Fargo listened to the coyotes singing and the whir of bats and owls as they hunted. No one had come. He'd arrived about an hour after moonrise and had been waiting a good two hours more.

Fargo pulled up the collar of his buckskin jacket as the desert wind turned colder. Whoever it was had either given up on him before he'd arrived or wasn't going to show. He was just beginning to wonder if he ought to ride on to Chimayò, when he saw it.

Movement. In the brush at the top of the hill. The Ovaro, hidden in the shadow of the rock, pawed nervously. Its keen nostrils had picked up the scent of something.

Yes, movement above on the hill. A figure walking in the brush. Then two, three. Fargo slid the Colt from its holster and the moonlight gleamed blue on the barrel. There was a long, wavering line of dark figures walking through sage, spread out across the hill as if searching, their heads bent low. As they came nearer, Fargo saw that they were all robed and hooded. Monks. He felt relief wash over him. He holstered his pistol and walked out to meet them.

His boots crunched on the gravel trail, and the line came to a halt. Fargo raised a hand in greeting as he neared.

"What are you looking for?" he called out.

There was a long silence, and then one of the monks stepped forward, his face hidden in the shadow beneath his cowl.

"Who are you?" the monk said gruffly.

Fargo suddenly felt a sensation of danger. Something was wrong. He must be on his guard his instincts told him. Fargo didn't hesitate a second.

"Name's Brent Barker, Father," Fargo said in a loud and friendly voice. He kept his head down under his low hat brim, his face hidden from the glare of moonlight. "Heading down to Santa Fe. I think I took a wrong turn. I'd be much obliged if you could tell me which way it is."

The monks stood in silence for a long moment. Then the rough voice answered him again.

"Turn around, stranger," the monk said. "Santa Fe's over that way. About fifteen miles." He pointed across the broken land toward the southeast.

"Thank you kindly," Fargo said, backing away. "Since it's so late, I guess I'll just camp here for the night and head out there in the morning." Maybe, he thought, whoever was supposed to meet him might still be coming.

"This is Tewa land," the monk said, his thick voice hard-edged. "And we've had some trouble out here. We don't like trespassers."

"Really?" Fargo said, keeping up the ruse of naivete. "I heard of the Tewa tribe. Now, are *you* Tewa?"

"This is Tewa land," the monk repeated sternly. Fargo saw the glint of a rifle emerge from the folds of the dark robe. "And we are from the Tewa Mission."

"I guess so," Fargo said. He returned to the shadow of Castle Rock and mounted the Ovaro. As he rode off, he turned and looked back. The dark figures of the monks were ranged across the hillside. They stood, silent and still, watching him ride off. Who ever heard of a monk toting a rifle? He wondered what connection they had with the stranger he was supposed to have met at Castle Rock. Maybe he could get that question answered by Padre Amado Fernandez at Chimayò.

He had gone scarcely a mile and was just galloping up out of a shallow arroyo when the Ovaro shied and nickered. Fargo knew the signal. The pinto sensed something out there in the darkness—something that didn't belong. Fargo reined in and sat for a long moment, looking about him, his senses alert. The pinto moved nervously under him. Then he heard a sound, so faint another man would have missed it.

Fargo dismounted, drew his Colt, and made his way through the brush and pale summer-dry grass. He heard the sound again. Unmistakable. A human noise, a moan. An instant later, he glimpsed a dark form—a man. Fargo glanced around, then bent over and turned him face up.

He was wearing a monk's robe. The moonlight fell across his face, which was badly disfigured. The nose had been smashed and the cheeks cut deep. Blood blackened his face so that Fargo could barely distinguish his features. The man tried to open his eyes and finally managed it. His lips parted, blood ran from his mouth, and Fargo heard the terrible moan again. Then he realized the man's tongue had been cut out.

"Take it easy," Fargo said, wondering if this was the man he was supposed to meet. He propped him against a rock. He didn't have long to live. That was for certain and there was nothing Fargo could do for him. Not even a drink of water would ease his suffering now.

"Who did this to you?" Fargo asked.

The man moaned and moved his head from side to side. Fargo felt his frustration. How could he communicate?

"I came to Castle Rock tonight to meet somebody," Fargo tried again. "Padre Amado Fernandez sent me."

At the padre's name, the man's eyes fluttered again and then fixed on Fargo's face with a look of sudden hope, terrible in its desperation. His hand stirred against Fargo and he moaned. Fargo felt the man trying to press something into his hand, and Fargo took it, then held it out into the moonlight. It was a length of rope, knotted rope.

"Is this a message?" Fargo asked. "For Amado Fernandez?" The dying man nodded slowly. His breath was strained now, rasping, and he brought his hands together, working. Fargo saw that he was trying to get his ring off his finger. Fargo removed the ring. Then the man's hand scrabbled at the soil and came up with a handful of it, pressing it into Fargo's hand. He breathed once, heavily, and then no more.

Fargo felt the dry earth trickling through his fingers

as he looked down at the dead man. The pinto nickered, almost silently. He glanced up to see the line of monks descending the slope. Swiftly, Fargo melted into the shadow of the nearby cutbank and pulled the Ovaro with him into the cover of thick brush. A few minutes later, he heard the sounds of the approaching men.

"Over here!" one shouted. Fargo peered out from the brush and saw the dark shapes of the robed monks gathering around the dead man. Maybe he could find out what this was all about. But they did not speak. They hoisted the corpse on their shoulders and then moved off. Fargo watched as the silent procession disappeared over the hill.

Fargo wondered at the strange monk with the rifle who had warned him off the Tewa land. The monks had been searching for the one who'd been tortured. To rescue him? Or to kill him? It had been impossible to tell. Amado Fernandez would have some answers. Fargo rode off into the night.

Dawn was primrose yellow as he reined in the Ovaro and sat looking down at the Sanctuario de Chimayò. All around, red rocks rose in weird formations. Here and there, black forms of rude wooden crosses marked the bare hillsides, stark against the brightening sky. Below in the center of a small cluster of adobe buildings stood the famous mission, its dun-colored walls softened by time and weather. Chickens scratched in the dust before the church. As he watched, a young boy ran across the yard and disappeared inside. The rusted iron bell in the tower began to move back and forth slowly and then pealed as the clapper hit the lip. The ringing sound, hollow in the cool morning air, resounded off the rocks. The doors to the nearby houses opened one by one, and rebozo-wrapped women and men in colorful cotton shirts headed toward the mission. When Fargo reached the churchyard, he dismounted. Through the open doors he could hear the voice of Padre Fernandez intoning a sermon.

Fargo spotted a trough and pump and led the Ovaro over to it. After the horse drank its fill, Fargo led it into the stable nearby. He filled a manger with fresh oats, found curry combs, and gave the horse a thorough brush-down while it munched at the feed. He had just finished and was closing the stall door behind him when he heard Padre Fernandez's voice.

"Fargo! You're here! I was getting worried."

Padre Amado Fernandez had changed in the five years since Fargo had last met up with him. Fernandez's thick wavy hair was grayer, the lines in his face etched more deeply, and his shoulders were stooped. And there was a sadness about him that Fargo had not seen before. The padre clapped him on the back.

"You didn't come in to hear my sermon?" At least Fernandez hadn't lost the old twinkle in his kindly brown eyes.

"I'm just not the praying kind," Fargo said.

"You never have been," the padre said with a laugh. "Don't ever tell the archbishop I said this, but sometimes I think some men don't have to be." Then the padre's face grew serious, and he looked around, concern in his face.

"But where is Lucero? Did you bring him to me? Did you get my message?"

"Yeah," Fargo said. Just then a flock of children came running up and surrounded Fernandez. They hopped up and down and tugged on his robe.

"Not now! Not now, my children," the padre said, shooing them gently away. Laughing and chattering like a flock of birds, the children ran off toward the parish garden. "Come inside and we will talk," Fernandez said, concern in his face.

The padre led the way past the small walled vegetable garden and through a narrow gate. They crossed a courtyard and entered a low door. Fargo found himself inside a simple whitewashed room. On one wall was a low rope bed with a blanket folded on one end and above it hung a crucifix. On the other wall was a bench and a table. A carved wooden chair stood toward the center of the room.

"Please," Padre Fernandez said, gesturing toward the chair as he seated himself on the bench. Fargo realized this was the padre's cell.

Amado Fernandez stared at the bare wall as Fargo told him about receiving the message in Taos and about the missed meeting at Castle Rock. His face took on a puzzled look when Fargo described the monks and the rifle he had glimpsed. When Fargo reached the part about finding the dying man, he retrieved the knotted rope and the ring from his pocket and handed them over. The padre took them and tears came to his eyes.

"This is Lucero's ring," he said, holding it up. "You see my initials here and the holy insignia. It was mine, but I gave it to Lucero as a token of our friendship. He said it would never leave his finger until he died."

"Who was this Lucero?"

"His given name was Thunder-Mountain," Fernandez said. "He is . . . *was* chief of the Tewa."

"Tewa? But he was dressed like a monk."

"Yes. That part of your story is a great mystery to me," the padre said as he shook his head. "Lucero was a good man. But more than that, he was a good Tewa. I know he continued to worship his Tewa gods too and—don't tell the archbishop this either—I did not condemn him or his people for that. But why he would be dressed as a monk—I just don't understand this."

"Maybe it wasn't Lucero after all. Maybe Lucero is still alive."

"No, I am certain it was Lucero," Fernandez said, shaking his head sadly. Because of this"—he held the ring aloft—"and because of what Lucero had told me. A month ago, he came to tell me that there was bad medicine at the Tewa Pueblo. But he could not explain what he meant. Then he sent a message. *Find someone to help*, it said. *Send him to me at moonrise and I will have the information about the danger.* So I sent for you. The padre paused and wiped his face anxiously. He held then the knotted rope aloft and stared at it, his brow furrowed with thought. "And now this is our only clue."

"It's some kind of signal," Fargo said. "Maybe how many knots there are. Looks like four."

"Yes, four," Fernandez said slowly, twisting the cord

slowly. "A knotted rope. This makes me think of something else, but I cannot remember what. I must meditate on this."

Fargo explained about the handful of earth that Lucero had tried to press into his palm, but the padre had no idea what that might mean either.

"And what about these monks?" Fargo asked.

A dark cloud passed over the padre's face. He rose and paced up and down on the stone floor and finally spoke.

"I am guilty of the sin of envy," the padre said, a touch anger in his voice. "Envy! The basest of emotions. And so it is difficult for me to speak of this new mission that has come to the Tewa just three months ago. Their leader is Claudio Gonzalez. I had never heard of him, but he appeared one day, sent by the bishops in Mexico. He set up a mission at Black Mesa."

"What's he like?"

"A powerful man," the padre said. "As was my custom on Wednesdays, I rode my burro up to the Tewa pueblo the week he arrived. I introduced myself to the brothers, and they kept me waiting for an hour until he had time to see me. Then they ushered me into the small chapel there—the chapel where I have always made the communion! There he sat by the altar. He is very quiet and he keeps his hood on at all times. He motioned me to come forward and take communion from him, which I did. I could hardly see his face, but what I saw was badly scarred, as if he had suffered some terrible trial. He asked me questions about everyone in the territory. And when he spoke, his voice was like the voice of God."

Fargo watched as the padre paced the room again, his hands twisting the length of knotted rope that he held. He was obviously fighting his emotions.

"What did he say?"

"Only that he had been called to minister to the Tewa flock," Padre Fernandez said. "He blessed me and told me that God would send me a vision. I felt his holy power, as if I were in the presence of God himself. And then the room began to . . . well, to change. And I saw snakes coming up from the floor." The padre paused, and his eyes took on a faraway look of remembering. "I have never told anyone this before. Not even my own confessor. Somehow I found myself on my burro going back to Chimayò and the way was filled with snakes. Everywhere. I knew it was a message from God. And I knew that I had failed. That these were the creatures of my envy, of my ambition, of my own weakness."

The padre hung his head.

"I think there's a rational explanation for this," Fargo said. "Those snakes were just your imagination. Maybe you were just tired."

"No," the padre said. "It was a mystical experience. I saw them, I tell you. And Gonzalez had told me I would have a vision from God. You see, he was right. He is touched by God."

"I don't accept that," Fargo snapped.

"God has even taken my Tewa away," the padre added. "They do not come to Chimayò anymore. They go to Gonzalez. He has many brothers to help him. His mission is now the most powerful in the territory."

"So who cut out Lucero's tongue?" Fargo asked.

"Maybe a Tewa," the padre said sadly. "Somebody jealous. Maybe Lucero had joined the brotherhood, and one of the Tewa felt betrayed and was threatening him."

"If that was the case, then Padre Gonzalez would have been able to stop it. And Lucero would have gone to him for help. I think this Padre Gonzalez wanted to keep Lucero quiet about something."

"Oh, certainly not!" Padre Fernandez said, his brows raised. "You will know when you meet him. Padre Gonzalez is a man of the cloth. He has taken holy vows. He is sacrificing his life to bring the word of God to this desert. No, I am certain that Gonzalez and the brothers are not involved in this affair. Besides, you yourself saw them looking for poor Lucero's body. No, I am certain there is some other answer to this murder."

"Then why was that monk carrying a rifle?"

Padre Fernandez paused for a moment.

"Yes, that is very strange," he agreed. "But maybe they are in danger, too. If the brothers are carrying rifles, there must be a good reason. I am sure they would not use them to kill, but only to frighten away whatever danger was near. Like whoever killed Lucero."

Fargo felt certain the padre was just being naive. "Maybe we should go up there and have a talk with Gonzalez," Fargo suggested.

"No, I cannot do that," Fernandez said sadly. "I am

no longer welcome on the Tewa land. The tribe does not welcome me. They listen only to Padre Gonzalez. They have asked me to stay away. Oh, maybe it is just my jealousy. Maybe I was wrong to call on you."

"No," Fargo said. "You're too hard on yourself, Padre. And this whole Gonzalez thing stinks."

The priest looked at him with surprise, a glimmer of hope in his eyes. But then he shook his head sadly. "Let us speak no more of it," he said. "You will rest today. Tonight we will dine together. My ward, Desideria, will join us tonight. She is in the convent at Santa Fe, and when she heard you were coming, she was most eager to meet you." There was that twinkle again in the padre's eyes.

Fargo rose, suddenly realizing how tired he was from the long night in the saddle. They made their way to the guest quarters where the padre showed Fargo his room and left to attend to the business of the mission.

The guest quarters were better appointed than the padre's bare cell. A comfortable feather bed was covered with crisp white sheets and colorful blankets. A china washstand, leather chairs, and a tall wooden chifforobe filled the room. Fargo brought his gear in from the stable, pulled off his boots, and lay down. Sleep came fast. His dreams were filled with the forms of monks and a writhing snake that turned into a knotted rope that untied itself, knot by knot.

Fargo awoke in late afternoon and found a small cold meal of tortillas and beans waiting for him on a tray. He ate, bathed, and walked outside. In the bare yard the chickens were pecking at the sun-cracked earth. Three barefoot boys lay propped against a cottonwood tree, dozing in the dappled shade. The iron bell was silent in the adobe tower. Fargo walked through the large wooden doors into the coolness of the sanctuary. On the dirt floor were rows of rude benches. Flickering candles lit the colorful pictures of saints in niches along the walls. Behind the simple cross at the altar was a carved wooden screen painted with images of birds and animals and flowers. A few people sat silently praying. Fargo heard the padre's voice and followed the sound into the room adjoining the sanctuary.

There Padre Fernandez was kneeling beside an old woman, binding her ankle with a bandage. Crutches and canes of various sizes and shapes were leaning against the walls all around the room. The padre looked up when Fargo entered.

"You see all the many people who have been healed here," the padre said, gesturing at the abandoned crutches. He finished binding the woman's ankle, got to his feet, fished around in his pocket, and then handed her a small packet. "Take these pills twice a day. And do not walk too much, señora. And pray. I am sure our Holy Father will make it better." The woman kissed the padre's hand and limped out of the room.

"Looks to me like you're the one making it better," Fargo said.

"A little medicine and a little faith work hand in hand," Padre Fernandez said. He glanced around the empty room, then picked up a bucket of earth that stood in a corner. "Come with me," he said and led the way to a small room toward the back. "Please stand at the door and tell me if anyone is coming."

Fargo did as he was told and then watched the padre kneel beside a small hole in the center of the dirt floor. He made the sign of the cross and then began carefully pouring the earth into the cavity.

"What are you doing?" Fargo asked.

"It is the healing mud," the padre explained as he worked. "Long ago, there was a spring on this place where the Indians came for healing. Then when the mission was built, people still came to take away a little of the moist earth for its curative properties. Only problem is, so many people come now, that I must always put some more earth here or the whole floor would soon disappear."

Fargo heard some voices and alerted the padre who quickly secreted the empty bucket, rose, blessed the room again, and dusted off his hands as they left. A family of four passed them and nodded to the padre as they made their way toward the small room. Once outside, the padre walked around the yard.

"Maybe you think it is wrong of me to put this earth back? Maybe you think I am fooling the people?" the padre said, distractedly.

"I think bandaging that woman's leg does more good than some holy mud," Fargo said.

"But sometimes medicine fails," the padre said. "And that is when people need something to believe in."

"Yeah, but other times people just think that believing will make everything come out all right. And then they don't act."

"Yes, Skye," the padre said with a laugh. "This is the difference between us. I am a man of faith. You are a man of action. Both of us righteous in our own ways."

The sound of approaching horses drew their attention. The padre's face brightened.

"That must be Desideria!" he said, his lined face wreathed in smiles. "The convent school has not allowed her to visit me at home for the last year. They are too strict, I think. So every week I go to see her in Santa Fe. But now she is coming home for a visit."

They watched as two palominos cantered toward them along the dusty road. Fargo made out the figures of two women as they came nearer and turned into the yard. The younger one, in a dark riding cape, reined in and jumped down from her horse. She came flying across the yard and embraced the padre. Behind her, the other woman, thin-faced and sallow, wearing a nun's habit, dismounted stiffly.

"Father!" the young woman said. "I am so glad to be home!" She took a step back from him and then turned to face the mission church. "Oh, I have missed Chimayò!" She whirled about suddenly and regarded Fargo. Her dark eyes flashed. She was beautiful, honey-skinned with thick, waving hair that fell to her waist and large black eyes that sparkled with intelligence and humor. As she gazed at him, she unbuttoned her cape and slid it off her shoulders and he noticed her slender waist, the full curves of her hips and, beneath her white blouse, the blooming fullness of her breasts. He raised his eyes to hers again and saw her blush.

Padre Fernandez cleared his throat.

"This is Skye Fargo," he said. "My ward, Desideria Fernandez y Aznar."

The young woman extended her hand to him, a grave look on her face but merriment in her eyes. "I have heard all about you, Mr. Trailsman," Desideria said. "All the girls at the convent—"

"That is quite enough, Desideria," the nun cut in, hurrying forward. She slapped the young woman's hand away from Fargo's. "I am Sister Alva. From the Convent School at Santa Fe. I am responsible for the señorita." Sister Alva glowered at Fargo with an expression that left no doubt in his mind what she meant. He noticed that Desideria turned away to suppress a giggle.

"Come in, Sister Alva," the padre said, trying to take her arm. "We'll leave the young people here. Let me show you to your quarters. You must be tired after your journey."

Sister Alva shook off his arm and resolutely took Desideria's arm, pulling her along.

"Yes, you can show *us* where we are sleeping tonight."

The padre shrugged and followed the two women. Desideria looked back and smiled at Fargo as he followed them all inside.

"This mission is a failure," Sister Alva said. "Everyone in Santa Fe knows that. Why you hardly have enough money for the candles. And from what I hear, nobody comes here anymore."

Padre Amado Fernandez put down his fork, picked

up the wine bottle, and poured himself a glass, his hand trembling slightly. Desideria looked down at her plate, her cheeks flushed red.

"I suppose you are going to tell me I ought to be more like Padre Gonzalez over at Black Mesa," the padre said.

"Exactly," Sister Alva responded. "Why, he's got great plans for the whole territory. He came to call on the Mother Superior just two weeks ago. I think he's come up with new ideas for the convent, too. Then he gave a sermon to the young ladies. Stupendous! Simply stupendous! A voice like thunder!"

"What did you think?" Fargo asked Desideria quietly.

The young woman shrugged and glanced guiltily over toward her guardian. Clearly, she also had been impressed with Padre Gonzalez, but her loyalty to her guardian kept her from admitting it.

"*And,*" Sister Alva said importantly, "Padre Gonzalez has a direct connection to . . . " She paused dramatically. "To Rome! Straight to the Pope! He showed Mother Superior a letter right from the Vatican! Can you imagine? Gonzalez knows the Pope. And he's right here in our territory. I tell you, Gonzalez is a godsend."

"Just what are they teaching you in that convent?" Fargo broke in. He was tired of Sister Alva's worshipful praise of Gonzalez.

"In the mornings Sister Margarita teaches us history and reading," Desideria said, flashing a smile at him. "Then Sister Gracia takes us outside and we learn about plants and animals, the sun and the stars. In the afternoons we sew."

"And what about catechism?" Sister Alva asked sharply.

"Oh, yes," Desideria said. "Sister Alva teaches us religion." Desideria paused, her dark eyes on him. "But I read everything I can," she said with a rush. "I so want to understand the world. I want to know everything and to learn what is out there. I want—"

"That is quite enough, Desideria," Sister Alva cut in. "It is not correct for a girl to have so many wants. You must do as the saints do and curb your desires. Remember the tree of knowledge in the Garden of Eden."

Desideria fell silent, but Fargo could see the anger blazing in her eyes. She had a hot temper barely held in check. He'd always liked women with spirit. And beneath her demure exterior, Fargo could sense that Desideria was pure spitfire. Sister Alva turned toward Padre Fernandez and began to talk about Gonzalez. Fargo reached under the table and lightly touched Desideria's knee. She started, then smiled and reached under the table to clasp his hand, entwining her warm fingers in his.

"More wine?" Fargo asked, filling her glass with his free hand. The padre and Sister Alva were engrossed in church gossip.

"I want to learn everything," Desideria said in a low voice. "You understand? Everything."

Under the table she pulled his hand along her thigh, upward until he felt her pressing his finger against the bunched skirt between her legs. Fargo was surprised by her boldness.

"I understand," he said with a smile.

"It is time we had our evening prayers, Desideria," Sister Alva announced, suddenly rising. Reluctantly, Desideria let go of his hand. Fargo rose as the two women left the room, then sat down again.

Padre Fernandez gazed after them, his face flushed. "My Desideria will never be a nun," he said. "Not in a hundred years. Don't tell the archbishop I said this, but if every woman was a nun, then there would be no more Catholics." He chuckled and unsteadily poured himself another glass of wine, spilling some on the table. Fargo saw that the padre, probably depressed by all the talk about Gonzalez, had had too much to drink. He suggested they turn in and helped the padre to his room.

"Maybe Sister Alva is right," Fernandez muttered as he staggered down the hall and then tripped. Fargo caught him and kept him from falling. "Maybe I am all washed up. Maybe God is trying to tell me that. I've sinned. Yes, I've sinned the sin of envy and this is my punishment."

After he left the padre, Fargo let himself into his room. The evening was chilly and he lit a fire in the round brick fireplace in one corner. Golden light flickered on the white walls. Fargo kicked off his boots and stripped off his shirt. He heard the creak of a door and the soft patter of feet on the stone floor of the hall. A moment later, his door was pushed open a few inches. The firelight caught the figure of Desideria clothed in a loose white gown, her long hair hanging down around her shoulders like a dark shawl.

"At the convent all the girls tell stories about you, Skye Fargo," Desideria said shyly. "Everyone knows about you. They say you know everything about love. And I want to learn. I want to know everything. Will you teach me?"

2

Desideria stood in the doorway in her white gown, lit by the firelight. Her large dark eyes traveled across his muscular chest and returned to his face. Fargo moved forward, pulled her into the room, and closed the door softly behind her.

"How did you get away from Sister Alva?" he whispered.

"She does not rest very well and takes some sleeping powder at bedtime," Desideria whispered back with a giggle. "So tonight, she had three portions! But just in case, I have come down the hall to get some water." She raised the empty water pitcher she carried in one hand and then put it down on the floor by the door.

"But you might poison Sister Alva," Fargo said.

"She'll be fine. We do this all the time at the convent," Desideria protested. "Whenever we want to sneak out."

"Sneak out?" Fargo said with a laugh. "Where do you go?"

"We put on our lace mantillas, which cover our faces so no one will recognize us. And then we go down to a cantina on the square. Usually somebody will buy us a drink. And we dance!" Her eyes were laughing. "That is real life! Not this life behind the convent walls. That is not for me." Her eyes searched his for a long moment. "And sometimes I find someone who wants to kiss me. You see, I have already learned to kiss."

Fargo put his arms around her and bent over her. Her lips were soft and warm. He gently inserted his tongue, and she opened, hesitatingly, then took his tongue into her mouth. He felt her heart pounding like a bird's as he held her fragrant softness close to him.

"Oh, oh," she breathed as she put her head on his chest. He held her and listened to her breathing, fast and hard. "I see what a kiss can be now. These boys, they did not know how. Please," she said, turning her face up to his. "More, please."

"You don't know what you're getting into," Fargo said, pushing her gently away.

"You think I am a child, perhaps," Desideria said. She stepped away from him. "But no. You mistake me, Skye Fargo." Her eyes were blazing with her quick temper. "I know what it is between men and women. I have read all the books, and I know how it is done, even though I do not have experience. And I know what the sisters teach us—it is a sin. But I do not believe that. And I know all about you. I have heard all the stories about the trails you have traveled and all the women you have loved. So, I want to learn everything there is to know about love. I want to know the hundred ways to please a man. Who would know better than you? And I want you to teach me."

Suddenly, Desideria reached down and gathered up her nightgown and pulled it off over her head. She stood before him, naked and bathed in the flickering light of the fire. her breasts, hard nippled with dark areolas, were full and heavy, round as large melons. Below her narrow waist, her smooth hips and soft belly, her dark triangle glistened. Fargo felt himself harden, throbbing with the desire to be inside her.

"You see, I am not a child," Desideria said.

"You know I'm not the marrying kind," Fargo said.

"I know all the stories about you," Desideria said. She crossed to him, and he took her in his arms, kissing her again deeply, his tongue deep in hers. His hands traveled down the deliciously silken curve of her long back and full hips. She gasped as they parted, and he bent to pick her up. He carried her toward the bed as she clung to him and lowered her gently onto the blanket. Her hand played in his hair as he kissed her breast, taking the nipple between his lips and tonguing it swiftly. She moaned and her fingers tightened in his hair.

"Oh, God," she breathed.

His hand traveled slowly downward across her rib cage and rounded belly, brushing across the curly nap and across her thighs, exploring her silken skin, slowly, slowly. She panted as he neared touching her, then stroked her elsewhere, teasing. Her hips began a rhythmic thrust, and her breath came in ragged panting until he began kissing a long trail across the soft curve of her belly, and then he parted her thighs and saw the pink folded wetness of her. He felt himself harden even more, eager to be inside her. He took her in his mouth and she sobbed in ecstasy, bucking under him uncontrollably.

"Ah, ah, my God!" she said, trying in vain not to make too much noise. He inserted one finger, then two, into her tightness, and felt her open up slowly. She gasped in pain and then in ecstasy as he flicked his tongue across her again, feeling her contract as she came, explosively, furiously, unable to hold back. She cried out, and Fargo wondered how long Sister Alva would sleep through all the ruckus. Hell, Desideria was a spitfire all right.

After a moment Fargo rose to his knees, unbuckled his belt, and stripped off his Levi's. His huge rod stood out, ready for her, and Desideria gasped. She reached out hesitatingly and then grasped it in her warm hand.

"Ah, it is so . . . so hard. So wonderful," she breathed. "Please, please put it inside me and teach me this."

She guided the tip of him to her portal, and he slowly, very slowly, eased inside her wetness as it stretched to accommodate the full length of him. Then he began to stroke slowly, back and forth, thrusting deeper and deeper into her tight sheath, feeling the throbbing urgency gathering in him. He moved his hips against her with every thrust, against her hard knot of desire, and she began to thrust upward to meet him.

"It is like riding," she gasped between breaths. "Yes, like my horse, but better!"

He felt her contract, her warmth holding him tighter as she writhed beneath him, her soft mounded breasts heaving. He covered them with his hands and thrust deeper and harder inside her wet warmth, feeling the gathering and then the fire that rose within him.

"Ah, yes, yes," she sobbed, bucking under him. Her fingers clutched his back and he let go, shooting his hotness hard into her, thrusting upward like a fountain spraying deep up into her, the throbbing, pumping again, again, again, until at last, he was spent and he fell forward onto her softness.

"Oh, Skye," she whispered after a time.

He lay beside her on the narrow bed, holding her close, his face buried in the tangles of her fragrant dark hair.

"Well, did you learn anything?" he asked, tickling her belly.

Desideria giggled.

"Yes, I learned how a man pleases a woman," she said. "But you did not teach me how a woman pleases a man. How to do maybe some other things . . ."

"That will be lesson number two," Fargo said, nuzzling her. "Are you ready?"

The sound of a crash and the breaking of glass came from the direction of the room where Sister Alva was sleeping. Desideria jumped out of the bed and struggled into her nightgown. She grabbed the water pitcher and let herself out into the hall. Fargo stood at the door and listened.

"Desideria?" It was Sister Alva's irritating voice, slurred with the sleeping potion. "Where is that girl?"

"Right here, Sister Alva!" Desideria answered. "I was just getting some water." Fargo heard the sound of the hand pump at the other end of the long hall. He heard their voices for another few minutes and the door closed again. Then he heard a strange scraping sound. Fargo tried to imagine what it was, then realized it was a piece of heavy furniture being dragged across the floor. Sister Alva was probably moving her bed to block the door since there were no locks at the mission. Desideria's second lesson would have to wait for another time. Fargo lay down and drifted off to sleep.

Padre Fernandez counted out the small white communion wafers as he put them into a cloth wallet and then dropped the wallet into the saddlebag on the burro. Fargo held the bridle of the burro while it flicked its long ears impatiently.

"I must always carry the communion with me wherever I go. Today I go to the mountains," the padre said, patting the rope-netted flask of wine hanging from the saddle. "I go to a small village that lost three children to influenza last week." He crossed himself. "I hope none of the other children are sick. So, I would be very grateful if you could escort Desideria and Sister Alva back to Santa Fe."

"Yeah," Fargo said. "And while I'm there, maybe I ought to report this murder to the sheriff and talk it over with him."

"Don't bother," the padre said. "It won't do any good. The sheriff's only interested in what happens in the town of Santa Fe. If it's Indian affairs, he figures it's none of his business. But you might pick up some gossip. Santa Fe is a talking town. Everybody talks about everybody else's business. There's a rumor running around there every ten minutes."

"Well, maybe I'll hear something about what's going on up at Black Mesa," Fargo said. "The problem is, I can't very well ride up to the Tewa Mission and ask who the hell killed Lucero."

"I suppose not," the padre said. He mounted the burro. "This isn't going to be easy, Fargo. But find out what you can."

After a moment the padre disappeared down the road, and Fargo heard the sharp voice of Sister Alva. She was leading Desideria through the vegetable garden.

"And as soon as we're back to the convent, you must go immediately to confession," the nun was saying. "This transgression cannot be tolerated, Desideria. It is a path that will lead you straight to hell, I promise." Sister Alva stopped short when she spotted Fargo.

"Mr. Fargo," she said coldly.

"Good morning, Skye," Desideria called out. Her cheeks were flushed, and her large black eyes gleamed with merriment and the secret they shared. Sister Alva looked suspiciously on the look that passed between them.

"The padre's gone into the mountains," Fargo said. "He asked me to escort you back to Santa Fe."

"The sooner the better," Sister Alva snapped. "I'll go get our things." She disappeared inside.

"What was that all about?" Fargo asked.

Desideria gave him a quick kiss, then rolled her eyes.

"I forgot to say my morning prayers!" She giggled, then grew serious when the nun appeared again, carrying two small bags. Fargo saddled the Ovaro and their two palominos. In a short time they were galloping through the hills, heading south toward Santa Fe. The red rock drifts were cut by wind and rain and in places looked like a molten flood. Some hills were dotted with dark piñons, others were bald dry earth. In the deep blue sky, the billowing clouds gathered in tall towers above the distant mesas. Fargo heard the rumble of far-off thunder, even though the morning sun shone brightly.

By midmorning, they reached the outskirts of Santa Fe. Fargo had been through the town many times before, but it had been several years ago. He doubted anyone would recognize him. But he well remembered the surrounding Presidio, the adobe wall that had protected the town from attack at one time. The winding narrow streets, the splendid many-storied adobes, and mud-brick hovels were all familiar sights. Red chile garlands, called *ristas,* swung from low eaves. Everywhere windows and door jambs were brushed with bright blue paint, believed to keep the devils out of the house.

Sister Alva led the way to the convent not far from the main square. The school was surrounded by a high adobe wall, breached by a tall wooden fence. They dismounted and Sister Alva called out. The gate opened slowly. Beyond it, Fargo glimpsed a pretty garden with a gurgling fountain and flowering vines hanging in profusion from wrought-iron balconies. Nuns and white-frocked young women walked around in the garden. An elderly woman in a severe black habit spotted them and came forward.

"Mother Superior!" Desideria called out. "I would like you to meet someone. This is Skye Fargo. He was visiting us—Father Fernando, I mean—at Chimayò."

The old woman's bright blue eyes narrowed as she regarded him. "So this is the famous Trailsman," she said, her voice sharp. Nevertheless, Fargo thought he caught a hint of humor in her eyes. "I hear you are very good. But also very dangerous."

"So, my reputation's got around," Fargo said with a smile.

"Yes, indeed," said the Mother Superior. Fargo saw she was finding it hard not to smile back at him, and she struggled to keep the severe look on her face. "But I hope you will do all your famous deeds outside this convent and not try to be a fox in our chicken coop." She shook her finger at him like a schoolmarm. Sister Alva blushed and cleared her throat, clearly mortified.

"I . . . I have to report that Desideria forgot her morning prayers, Mother," Sister Alva said.

The Mother Superior held up her hands. "I am sure she can make up for that later. Come in, my child." Desideria smiled at Fargo as Sister Alva escorted her into the garden. "Mr. Fargo," the Mother Superior said. "I wonder if you would step into my office for a moment. I have a proposition to put to you."

"Sure," Fargo said. "I've never been propositioned by a Mother Superior before."

The old nun laughed merrily, and Sister Alva gasped, pulling Desideria with her. Hell, he had never had an offer from a Mother Superior before, he thought to himself. Curious as to what was on her mind, Fargo tethered the Ovaro and followed her inside the gate, which closed behind him. At once, the women in the garden fell silent, and he felt their eyes on him. The sound of his heeled boots on the stone was the only sound besides the gurgle of the fountain. Two dozen women stood in knots around the garden—some in black nuns' habits, others in the white frocks of the students. Some were slender and tall, others round and petite. Blondes, brunettes, redheads, he smiled at them all as the Mother Superior led him toward the convent. Some smiled back. Others blushed and turned away. Desideria looked longingly at him over her shoulder as Sister Alva pulled her away in the opposite direction.

Mother Superior ushered him inside. She took a seat behind an ornately carved table and gestured for him to seat himself. The nun looked at him in silence for a long moment.

"Yes, Mr. Fargo. I know your reputation," she began. "But I've also heard you're a good man. An honest man. Right now, I need an honest man. It's about Padre Fernandez. Have you . . . known him long?"

"Met him years ago out in California," Fargo said. "He did a damn good job out there."

The Mother Superior pursed her lips and shook

her head thoughtfully. "So I've heard," she muttered. "But things have changed. In the last few weeks I have begun to receive complaints from the bishop in Mexico about his behavior. Drunkenness. Debauchery. Stealing from the coffers—"

"Now, hold on a minute," Fargo said. "The padre may have a little too much wine every once in a while, but the rest of it? Women? Stealing? He's not the type. I know Padre Fernandez well enough to know that's not his style."

"I thought I knew him well also," the nun said thoughtfully. "That was my first reaction. But you see, God has taken away his flock. So, these things must be true. It is a punishment from God. All the Tewa Indians that used to go to Chimayò are going elsewhere."

"You mean to Black Mesa. To Padre Gonzalez."

"You know Father Gonzalez?" the nun asked, a note of excitement in her voice.

"Never met the man," Fargo said. "But everything I hear about him makes me suspicious. And as to these letters from that bishop in Mexico about Padre Fernandez, did you ever ask yourself where that bishop got his information? How does somebody down in Mexico know so much about what's going on up at Chimayò?"

"No," the Mother Superior said slowly. "No, I didn't think of that."

"The whole thing sounds like a frame-up to me," Fargo said. "Some kind of plot to discredit Padre Fernandez. But why?"

"And who?" the nun said.

"Gonzalez is behind it," Fargo said. "That's obvious."

"Oh, come now," she said. "Padre Gonzalez? Why, he's one of the most respected brothers in the entire Church. The man is incredible. If you had ever met him, you couldn't say such a thing. Why, he's . . . he's touched by God."

"Yeah," Fargo said doubtfully. "Everybody seems to think so."

"You have no idea how important and powerful a man Padre Gonzalez is," the Mother Superior said. "Why, he even communications personally with our Holy Father in Rome." She crossed herself.

Fargo saw that it was useless. Nothing he could say would convince her that Padre Gonzalez might not be the paragon of virtue that she seemed to think he was. Fargo suspected the priest had gone bad and was plotting to get Padre Fernandez out of the territory. That kind of backroom finagling and power-grabbing had gone on in the Church and every other organization throughout history. So, what could he do about it? As he asked himself that question, Fargo knew there was something else wrong here. And it was bigger than just one priest trying to grab a congregation from another priest. It was bigger than one dead Tewa with his tongue cut out. And all his suspicions led straight to Gonzalez.

"Well," the nun said after a long moment of silence. "I see you're not going to be any help to me in what I need to have done."

"And what's that?" Fargo asked.

"To keep an eye on Padre Fernandez," she said. "If

the bishop of Mexico is right, then something must be done about the situation."

"Like having Gonzalez take over at Chimayò?"

"Certainly. The post at Chimayò is one of the most important on the continent. Many of the faithful make pilgrimages to be healed at Chimayò. I've already suggested to Padre Gonzalez that he take over there," the Mother Superior said, "but he flatly refused. He said he had his hands full with all the duties up at Black Mesa. So you see, Mr. Fargo, Padre Gonzalez is not ambitious. He is not trying to take over from Padre Fernandez. No, you are wrong."

So Gonzalez didn't want to take over the mission from Fernandez. But still, Fargo thought, Gonzalez was behind the smear campaign against the old father. But why? What did he stand to gain? What could Padre Gonzalez possibly have up his sleeve?

"Look, I'll keep my eyes open," Fargo said at last. "But I have to ask you something in return. Don't tell anybody I'm in town. Or that we spoke. Not Gonzalez. Not anybody. Don't use my name. I have my reasons. And pass the word to your ... your nuns, too. And all the girls."

The Mother Superior looked surprised for a moment.

"All right," she said.

"And get this straight," Fargo said. "I'll keep my ears open, but I'm not going to spy on Padre Fernandez for you. I've told you already, I know you're wrong about him. The bishop's wrong, too."

The nun sat silently, her bright blue eyes searching

his face. Then she stood and gestured him toward the door.

"I know in my heart you are right," she said as they bid good-bye. "But I must be sure."

As Fargo crossed the courtyard, Desideria came running toward him, followed closely by Sister Alva.

"Good-bye, Skye," Desideria said, extending her hand to shake his. Her dark eyebrows arched, and she gazed at him meaningfully as if signaling him. Fargo saw a scrap of paper secreted in her palm, and as he shook her hand, he took it and pocketed it.

"See you again," he said with a smile. He touched his hat brim to Sister Alva as she let him out of the gate. The heavy doors slammed shut behind him. Fargo took out the slip of paper and read the words: *Meet me tonight at the cantina. Midnight.* Fargo smiled to himself. Spitfire for sure. And courting danger at every turn.

The afternoon sun beat down. He headed through the narrow streets between the rounded adobe walls toward the main square. Fargo paused a moment in the shade, leaned against a cool adobe wall, pulled his hat down low over his eyes and surveyed the busy scene in front of him.

The town was the final destination on the famous Santa Fe Trail. All day long, year in and year out, heavy mountain wagons rumbled through the streets, the drivers and oxen exhausted and dusty after the long, hard journey. Crates and barrels of goods were being unloaded, and buyers and sellers crowded the open market area where traders and Indians sold their wares. Surrounding the square were public buildings, bars, restaurants, and an inn, or what the Mexicans called a *fonda*.

Fargo's attention was drawn by a wiry figure, an Indian in a belted brown smock who strode back and forth along the long line of Tewa men who sat crosslegged on the ground behind piles of pottery and folded woven blankets. The skinny man seemed to be keeping watch over his fellow Tewa. A white woman decked out in gingham approached and picked up one of the pieces of pottery and turned it in her hands, considering. The skinny man hurried over and seemed to do the negotiating, then pocketed the money she handed over for the pot. The Tewa sitting on the ground seemed to hardly notice, but sat as if dazed, staring straight ahead. As Fargo watched, he saw the scene repeated time and again. The skinny Indian was the one who did the bartering and pocketed the money as the others sat impassively. It seemed odd to Fargo, knowing how much Indians usually enjoyed the sport of barter, usually getting more pleasure out of the negotiation than the payment.

Just then, he spotted a priest emerging from the Governor's Palace, a long, low adobe building across the square where all the municipal officials did their business. For some reason the figure drew his attention. The robed man was tall and walked with purpose. His hood was up, and his face completely hidden. Fargo knew he was looking at the mysterious Padre Gonzalez.

Gonzalez was followed by a matching pair of monks built like grizzly bears, massive and powerful.

Fargo watched as the priest and the two monks crossed the square. They were hailed by a portly man in a big coffee-colored hat, and they stopped to talk to him. The sunlight glinted on a star on the man's chest, and Fargo saw it was the sheriff. He seemed to be very friendly with Gonzalez. Everybody seemed to be impressed by the new priest. The sheriff moved off, and the three men headed toward the Tewa Indians. For a few minutes they talked to the skinny man, then walked off toward a hitching post where a line of horses stood. They mounted and galloped off.

For a moment Fargo considered going to talk to the Tewa, but he didn't like the looks of the skinny fellow. Better not to show his own face, he decided. Not yet. For the moment he'd stay incognito. Instead, he made his way through the rumbling wagons and crowded streets around the square toward the Governor's Palace.

Inside a whitewashed room piled with boxes of papers, a harried-looking clerk sat furiously copying a document, his feather quill bobbing.

"What is it?" the clerk asked impatiently, not bothering to look up.

"Just got a question," Fargo said.

"Yeah." The clerk continued writing. Fargo turned over in his mind how to find out what he needed to know without arousing the clerk's suspicion.

"Were you able to help Padre Gonzalez with his problem?" Fargo asked.

"Oh, yeah," the clerk muttered distractedly. "I told him the circuit judge would be here in four days. The padre wanted a spot on the docket at noon on Friday, August fourth."

Why in hell did Gonzalez want an appointment with the circuit judge? Why would a priest need a civil court? Church affairs were always decided internally. The clerk glanced up, his brows lowered and a question on his face.

"But hey, who are you anyway?"

"Just wanted to make sure the padre was getting what he needed," Fargo said over his shoulder as he left the office. He didn't want the clerk to get too good a look at him or get too nosy. There was no way to find out more from the clerk now without raising more suspicion. And the last thing Fargo wanted was for word to get back to Gonzalez that somebody had been asking questions about him.

As Fargo rode the Ovaro back to Chimayò, he pondered the strange turn of events and thought about the tall hooded figure of Gonzalez. How could he get close enough to the padre to find out what was going on? The late afternoon sun was burnishing the high clouds when the mission came into view. In front of the church stood a small wagon with tin pots and utensils hanging off all sides.

As Fargo dismounted, a short, burly man with iron gray hair rounded the wagon and spotted him.

"Howdy!" the man said, coming up and shaking his hand. He spoke loudly. "Name's Robin Plowright. Smithy."

"Skye Fargo."

"Eh?" Plowright said. He put his finger in one ear.

"Didn't catch that, stranger. I'm a little hard of hearing, what with all the ringing on my anvil."

Fargo started to introduce himself again when Padre Fernandez hurried out of the mission. "Robin!" he called out in a very loud voice, obviously aware of the smithy's hearing problem. "I see you've met Skye."

"Pleased to meet you, Sty," Plowright said loudly, pumping his hand again. Fargo decided not to correct the old man.

Over dinner, Fernandez and Plowright talked about the doings in the valley while Fargo sat lost in thought. The itinerant smithy had been traveling the trails for years, going from town to town and pueblo to pueblo, shoeing horses, refitting wheel rims, and repairing pots and pans. He and the father traded gossip and news about people from Denver City all the way down to Mexico.

"But one thing I will say. It sure is a lot safer around here since that marshal ran down that old bandido, Carlos Juarez," Plowright said.

The name of Carlos Juarez brought Fargo out of his reverie. It was a name that had been feared throughout the West for more than a decade. Juarez and the No-Hand Gang had been the most violent, bloodthirsty bandidos in the territory. They had robbed wagon trains and stagecoaches, butchered men, women, and children. The gang got its name from the grisly custom of cutting off the right hands of their victims before killing them. Nobody ever figured out just why.

"Yep," Plowright continued. "Used to be a lot more

dangerous out there when Carlos Juarez was around. That was back four years ago already. Course you weren't around here then," he added nodding to the padre.

"I once ran into Juarez," the padre said, speaking loudly so Plowright could hear. "Back when he was just getting started out in California. He tried to steal the collection plate one Sunday, but we caught him at it. Ran him out of town."

"Too bad you didn't know then what he was going to turn into," Plowright said. "You could of hung him and saved the world a lot of misery. Y'ever hear how they caught old Carlos Juarez?" Plowright asked, turning to Fargo.

"Yeah," Fargo said.

"Well then, I'll tell you," Plowright said, not hearing Fargo's answer. The padre and Fargo exchanged smiles as the smithy launched into the story Fargo knew well from the newspaper stories and from dozens of accounts he'd heard during his travels. At the height of their criminal careers Carlos Juarez and the One-Hand Gang had wandered into Durango and, in the course of robbing the bank and shooting up the town, killed the mayor. The mayor's brother, a federal marshal by the name of McMullen, swore revenge. For the next three years he did nothing but dog Carlos Juarez and the One-Hand Gang, always just one step behind.

"Now, I never did meet old McMullen," Plowright said, "but I heard he was something fierce. And finally, one day, he caught 'em up in the Rio Grande canyon just north of here. Ole McMullen got a couple dozen men in a posse, and they backed that gang into a blind canyon. Then they poured in firepower until there were so many bullets flying around a mosquito would have been cut to shreds. Went on for hours. And at the end of that firefight, there was only one bandit left shooting. And then the marshal sees a white handkerchief on a stick. And he calls a halt to the firing. And you know what happened?"

Plowright paused dramatically and, even though Fargo knew the tale, he shook his head as if he didn't.

"Hell, Carlos Juarez himself staggers out of that bloody canyon all shot up and bleeding like a fountain, and he pitches right off that cliff and lands smack dab in the Rio Grande. Well, it was springtime, and I don't need to tell you that water was raging white against those rocks. Why that bandido's body was so pulverized they never did find it even though old McMullen looked and looked. So they strung up the rest of the One-Hand Gang in a nice row in downtown Santa Fe. That was a pretty sight."

Plowright paused and picked up his mug of beer.

"Now, what do you think of that story, Sty?" he said.

"It's *Skye*," the padre corrected him. "*Skye Fargo*."

Plowright's jaw fell, and he dropped the mug of beer heavily on the table. "*You're* Skye Fargo?" he said. "I've heard of you. And I heard your name real recently." Plowright scratched the stubble on his chin. "Oh, yeah. On the road from Taos. Some big guy. Tall fellow all in black on a pretty chestnut. Stopped and asked me if I'd seen or heard tell of you. Said he'd heard you headed down to Santa Fe. Was real eager to find you. Looked mad as hell when I said no. He rode off like a hundred devils were after him."

The man in black he'd seen in Taos, Fargo thought. Somehow he'd picked up his trail and followed him to Santa Fe. Who was he, anyway?

"Sounds like you made an enemy somewheres along the line," Plowright said. "He looked pretty mean. You ought to watch your back."

"Guess so," Fargo said, remembering the tall stranger's broken nose and dark, wary eyes.

"As for me, I'm going to be pushing off tomorrow," Plowright said. "Going up to Black Mesa for a spell. Always got some good customers up there. Check on ole Lucero."

"Lucero's dead," Padre Fernandez said. "And you'll find the whole pueblo is different." He told the old smithy all about Lucero's message, about Fargo coming to help and finding the dying man.

"I don't like the sound of this one bit," Plowright said hotly. "Lucero was a good Tewa. Good leader. Nobody would have a reason to torture and murder him. Hell, that burns me up." Plowright took a swig of beer and slammed down his mug.

"Lucero left this behind," the padre said, drawing the short length of knotted rope from a pocket in his robe.

"One, two, four knots," Plowright counted thoughtfully. "I guess that must mean something. Like four men? Four horses? Four days?"

Fargo felt his mind reel. Four days. Of course. The clerk had said it would be four days until the circuit judge arrived in Santa Fe. And that was when Padre Gonzalez had an appointment in court. Four days, four knots. The fourth of August. Or was that all just a coincidence?

"Four days," Padre Fernandez said thoughtfully. He suddenly slapped his forehead. "Now I remember what that reminds me of. The time the Taos pueblo rose up against the Spanish rulers. They sent Indian runners with knotted ropes. Every day a knot was untied, and when all the knots were removed, it was time to strike."

"Strike? Strike who?" Plowright asked.

"Maybe it's a message to us to attack the pueblo in four days," Fargo mused.

"Eh?" Plowright said. Fargo repeated himself louder.

"Only we can't attack the pueblo before we know what's going on up there," Fargo added.

"And I'm no longer welcome at the pueblo," Padre Fernandez said. "Neither are strangers." He nodded toward Fargo.

"But I am," Plowright said.

"And I'll bet you need an assistant," Fargo said, slapping the old man on the back. "Somebody to come with you to Black Mesa." The old man looked puzzled for an instant, then he brightened.

"Yeah, that's right," Plowright said with a wide grin. "I need an assistant. Getting old, you know." Plowright leaned over and felt Fargo's biceps. "I bet you'd be right handy with a forge and an anvil."

Yes, this would work nicely, Fargo thought. He would accompany Plowright to Black Mesa, and they would set up smithing for a few days. That would give him plenty of time to find out what was going on, who had killed Lucero, and why.

"An excellent plan," said the padre, raising his glass of wine. "Here's to success."

"Well, we oughta have a little music," Plowright said. "I'll fetch my one-man band." The smithy was back in a moment with a harmonica, a tambourine, and a mallet with some kind of spring apparatus attached. He fiddled with it, then set the tambourine in a special stand on the floor and stepped on the small foot pedal. The mallet hit the tambourine a few times, and then Plowright began to play a tune.

It took a while for Fargo to recognize the tune. Plowright was not only hard of hearing, but he was tone-deaf as well. Fargo smiled and got up to leave.

"I promised a lady I'd meet her in Santa Fe," he said as he left the room. He heard Padre Fernandez's chuckle, and then the painful music started up again. The priest was definitely a saint, Fargo thought.

Far be it from him to keep a lady waiting. By midnight Fargo sat in one corner of the cantina, his hat brim pulled low over his eyes, whiskey in hand, watching the crowd, a mix of trail bosses, local ranchers, and wandering cowpoke types. Nobody gave him a second glance.

A few minutes later, they swept in, a bevy of lithe young women in colorful dresses, their lace mantillas hiding their faces. As soon as they appeared, the men in the bar raised a shout and crowded around them. Fargo spotted Desideria immediately, in a rich purple dress cut low to show her deep cleavage, heavy black lace hanging in folds over her face. She pushed through the boisterous crowd of men, ignoring their invitations and offers for drinks as she made her way to the corner where Fargo sat waiting at an empty table.

"Is this seat taken?" she asked coyly. Even the black lace could not hide her eyes, glittering like black diamonds. He ordered her a drink and scanned the room. A few of the men scowled enviously at him. Better not to draw too much attention to himself, he thought, in case someone from the pueblo happened to be in the cantina and might recognize him later.

"Is there somewhere we can be alone?" he asked.

Desideria led him to a small private alcove with a curtain and a small window overlooking the alley behind the cantina. They settled in, and Fargo took her hand. Desideria pulled up her mantilla and he kissed her, deep and long. Her mouth was sweet, warm, hungry, and her tongue caressed his mouth, insistent.

"You've been practicing," he accused her.

"I have not!" she protested with a delighted laugh. He put his arm around her. "Oh, I can sneak out every night and we can meet here just like this."

"Actually, we can't. I'll be away a few days," Fargo said. "I'm going up to Black Mesa."

"To visit Padre Gonzalez?" Desideria asked with interest.

"Not exactly," Fargo said. "And nobody should know I've been in town. Did the Mother Superior tell you all not to say you'd seen me?" Desideria nodded, her eyes serious.

"Then, you're in danger?" she said, worry in her voice.

"Let's just say it complicates things if word gets around that I'm in Santa Fe."

Fargo pushed back the curtain and leaned forward to signal the bartender for another drink. By the bar he spotted a familiar figure. The tall man in black. Fargo leaned back and watched. The man seemed to be asking a man at the bar a question. The man shook his head, and the mysterious stranger moved on to the next and then the next. Fargo knew exactly what was happening. Just then one of the other girls came over.

"Oh," she said sounding scared. "Mr. Fargo, that man . . . that man—"

"Is asking about me," Fargo said. "Yeah, I know."

For a moment he considered his options. A confrontation in a crowded bar was dangerous. If the man in black had murder on his mind and they shot it out, they might kill some innocent bystanders. He'd rather have it out with the stranger one to one. Try to find out who he was.

Fargo made up his mind. He pulled the curtain shut across the opening of the alcove and inched the window sash upward. With a quick kiss good-bye and a promise to call on her when he returned from Black Mesa, Fargo jumped down into the deserted alley. Desideria shut the window behind him. Fargo circled the cantina and cut across the square. He leaned against a cottonwood tree where he had a good view of the front of the cantina and he waited. A half hour later, the five young women left in a giggling group, heading back to the convent. A few minutes after that, Fargo saw the tall stranger emerge.

The man stood for a long moment, gazing around the square, and Fargo shrank back into the shadows, then followed silently and at a distance as the man walked away. Fargo followed through the narrow, dark streets. He saw the stranger disappear around a corner. Fargo cautiously edged up to the corner of the building and looked down the street. There was no one in sight.

Suddenly, he heard the bare whisper of a sound and he tensed, but just then a heavy blow struck him across the back of the skull. The world spun and stars burst before his eyes. Fargo desperately tried to hold on to consciousness as he reeled and staggered, his hand on the butt of his Colt.

3

Fargo felt his knees buckle under him as the dark street wavered before his eyes. He gritted his teeth and gripped harder on the butt of his Colt. He had to hold on.

Powerful hands gripped his shoulders, spun him around, and pushed him hard against the adobe wall. Fargo felt the anger well in him as he found himself face-to-face with the tall stranger.

"Why are you tailing me?" the man asked, shaking him roughly.

"Who are you?" Fargo spat back.

In a split second Fargo wrenched himself free of the man's iron grip and brought a powerful fist into the man's solid belly. The stranger wheezed and staggered a step. Fargo followed with a hard uppercut that snapped the man's head back. He reeled and came around, eyes blazing and his long-barreled pistol in his right hand. Fargo leapt aside as it spat fire and the bullet whizzed by him with a nasty whine. He dove for cover behind a low adobe wall and then looked out, Colt in hand, searching the darkness for his mysterious assailant. A second shot told him where the man in black was hiding. The bullet ricocheted inches from his head.

The stranger was hunkered down behind a pile of barrels on the other side of the alley. Fargo heard voices shouting from a nearby street. They seemed to be heading his way. Suddenly, he noticed a tower of crates looming just above where the stranger was hiding. The crates were flimsy and stacked precariously. On top of them were a couple of heavy barrels. Fargo raised the Colt and fired, one shot after another, aiming for a flimsy crate just over where the man was hiding. As he hoped, the wood splintered under the hail of bullets, and the tower of crates and barrels came crashing down. Fargo, Colt in hand, leapt out from behind the wall and cautiously headed toward the pile of broken wood. He caught sight of a black boot emerging from the pile of wood. He kicked it hard. The man didn't move. He was out cold.

"This way! This way!" Fargo heard the voices approaching. Somebody was coming to find out what all the shooting was about. There was no time to lose.

Fargo pulled the unconscious man free of the rubble. A deep cut ran down one cheek, and Fargo could see the egg growing on his forehead. But he was still breathing. Swiftly, Fargo bent down and began searching through his pockets. A wallet with greenbacks. A buckskin poke full of silver coins. He dropped them on the ground. A packet of tobacco and rolling papers. A flint. Nothing to tell him who the stranger was.

"Yeah! Two shots! Over here, I think." The voices were coming nearer.

Fargo reached inside the man's vest pocket and felt a hard rectangle. He pulled it out. A small flat silver case.

"Hey! Hey you!" Fargo glanced up. The sheriff and a couple of men stood at one end of the alley.

"Thief! Thief!" one of them called out. Before Fargo could protest, the sheriff drew his pistol and fired. Fargo dove sideways, and the bullet zinged by him. He scrambled to his feet and vaulted over a high wall as he heard the spatter of bullets hit the adobe where he'd just been. He sprinted across the small courtyard to a low wooden door and let himself out onto the side street, then ran for another block, before turning into an alley and doubling back toward the town square where the Ovaro was tethered. Behind him he heard the men shouting and the occasional pop of gunfire, but he had thrown them off his trail. When he reached the square, he slowed his steps, walked calmly toward the pinto and mounted.

He could hear the sheriff and his men coming nearer to the main plaza. A couple of men walking by heard the approaching cacophony and paused.

"What's going on?" one of them called out to Fargo.

"I dunno," Fargo said nonchalantly. "I saw some guy running off that direction." He jerked his thumb over his shoulder and slowly eased the pinto in a slow walk toward a street leading in the opposite direction. He had just got out of sight around the corner of the hotel when he heard the voices of his pursuers as they burst onto the square.

"Somebody saw him go thataway!" a voice called out excitedly.

"That way!"

Fargo smiled to himself and then gently nudged the Ovaro into a gentle canter as they headed through the deserted streets of Santa Fe and out into the open country on the way back to Chimayò. After a few miles he paused at the edge of a stand of willows and watched the trail behind him. No one was following. He pulled the flat silver case from his pocket and saw the disc of moon reflected in its surface. The little case was too skinny for cigarettes. Fargo wondered what could be inside as he found the catch and opened it.

He withdrew its contents, a yellowed slip of paper, folded twice—a newspaper clipping. He had to strain his eyes to make out what was on it. And then he saw. A faded drawing of the One-Hand Gang, a sketch of the long line of limp bodies hung on ropes as they had been displayed in Santa Fe after the death of their leader, Carlos Juarez. Although he couldn't see the details in the dim light, Fargo remembered the drawing well. It had been printed and reprinted in newspapers around the country, and it showed the bloodied death-dark swollen faces of the notorious gang and the gleeful citizens parading by to look.

Now why would a man be carrying around a picture like that, Fargo wondered as he galloped toward Chimayò. He could think of several reasons. And he didn't like any one of them.

Robin Plowright's wagon creaked and groaned and clattered as it bumped along the trail, the hanging tin utensils and pots banging together each time the wheels hit a rut. Fargo, dressed in a smithy's leather apron and leggings, sat beside Plowright on the seat. The Ovaro was hitched in with Plowright's old mare and occasionally glanced back impatiently at Fargo and pawed the ground as if the wagon were too slow. The pinto didn't take well to drawing wagons, Fargo thought. It was too proud an animal, too fast and independent for the traces. But he and Plowright had decided it would look less suspicious this way. Everything depended on convincing the pueblo that he was Plowright's assistant.

All around, the vast land rolled under them, broken here and there with outcroppings of red rock and patches of gray sage and rabbitbrush. As they neared Black Mesa, it loomed higher and higher, seeming to fill the sky, a gigantic butte standing all by itself a short distance from the mountains which rose at the western edge of the plateau. Fargo gazed up at the magnificent hulking rock and thought he saw a flicker of movement along the top edge. But when he looked again, it was gone.

"What's up there?" he shouted to Plowright over the creak of the wagon.

"I heard tell there's just some old Indian ruins," the smithy shouted back. "S'posed to be a holy place for the Tewa."

They were coming up on Castle Rock, the small yellow promontory where Fargo found Lucero. They passed the rock and Fargo scanned the ground, recognizing the place where he'd hidden and watched the monks carry off the dead man's body. A mile down the road, they passed the spot where he'd waited in vain that night for Lucero to show up.

"We've crossed into Tewa land," Plowright announced. "All around here and for a good piece north and into the mountains belongs to the tribe. Biggest piece of Indian land in the territory. And they got some rich turquoise mining up there in the hills."

"Nice property," Fargo said idly. He suddenly stiffened and threw his arm across Plowright, knocking the man sideways. A bullet smashed into the wooden seat where the old man had been sitting an instant before.

"Hell!" Plowright shouted.

"Hold your fire!" Fargo called out.

"Get your hands in the air!" a gravelly voice shouted. A powerfully built man in a brown monk's robe stepped out from behind a rock just ahead, rifle in hand, the barrel pointed straight at them. Fargo and Plowright raised their hands slowly.

Fargo heard a step on gravel behind them and a second monk appeared. He recognized the two of them as the men he'd seen accompanying Padre Gonzalez in Santa Fe the day before. Fargo studied the two men's faces, weather-worn with flint-hard eyes and grim mouths. The only thing monklike were their robes. As they had planned, Plowright did the talking.

"Who are you? What's going on here?" the smithy said. "I'm heading up to the Tewa pueblo."

"Oh no you're not," one of the monks replied. "Turn right around and get out."

"Now, just a cotton-pickin' minute," Plowright said

hotly. "This is a free country. I can come and go as I please, and I been coming up to this pueblo for fifteen years. I ain't having nobody tell me I can't. Why those Tewa are expecting me. I always come around this time every summer and stay about a week."

"Who are you?" one said, lowering his rifle an inch.

"Robin Plowright," he said. "Smithy, iron master, tin repair. Shoe your horse, sharpen your knives. And this here's my assistant, Sty Foster."

Fargo nodded curtly to the two monks, who looked doubtfully at one another. "Well, all right. But gimme your sidearms," one said, approaching the wagon. "No guns allowed on this reservation." For a moment Fargo considered refusing, but he saw that that would just get them thrown off the reservation. He reluctantly handed over his Colt and his Henry repeating rifle and watched as they were stowed in one of the monk's saddlebags. At least he still had the blade strapped to his ankle.

"We'll have to take you to see the Padre," the other monk said. "He'll decide if you can stay."

The two monks brought out horses from behind some rocks, mounted, and one led the way while the other followed. Whatever was going on at the pueblo, Fargo thought, they sure did want to keep it a secret.

Fifteen minutes later, they arrived at the pueblo, a cluster of low adobe dwellings. As the wagon jounced along the dusty streets, the pueblo seemed deserted. In the heat of the day few Tewa were outside. Two women walked dispiritedly down a side street, carrying a large jug of sloshing water between them. A dog slept in the shade of a gnarled cottonwood. They reached the central plaza, a large open space where Fargo spotted the round shape of a sacred kiva with ladders leaning against its formidable walls. Not far away, the sheer sides of Black Mesa rose almost straight up into the air.

They came to a halt, and Plowright scrambled down from the wagon. Fargo followed deferentially, trying to remain inconspicuous and play the part of the assistant. The two monks led them toward the adobe chapel that stood to one side of the main square. Inside, the air was cool and musty. Fargo's eyes took a moment to adjust to the gloom.

At one end of the chapel, sitting on the raised platform in a gigantic carved chair in front of a large table, sat the hooded figure of Padre Claudio Gonzalez. He was writing something with a quill pen. He glanced up and laid his pen down carefully. He rose and Fargo was struck once again by the powerful presence of the man. He moved with a kind of majesty and force that drew attention immediately. Padre Gonzalez halted and stood at the edge of the dais.

"Approach," he said. His resonant voice echoed through the empty chapel. Plowright swallowed hard and went forward. Fargo followed warily.

They stopped and stood side by side. Fargo tried to see the padre's face, but it was hidden in the shadow of his hood, as if the man were faceless. His shoulders were broad and he was tall. But he was completely hidden by his robe, and all that could be seen were his powerful hands, which seemed, in the half light, to be wrinkled with age or scarred with hard living.

"I'm Robin Plowright," the smithy said again, repeating the explanation of why they were there. Fargo heard the nervousness in the old man's voice. The sight of the powerful padre had clearly affected Plowright. But somehow, as the smithy spoke, Fargo felt the padre's eyes were fixed on him. He felt the cold, hard, curious stare of Gonzalez from the darkness inside the hood, and he tried to keep his thoughts off his face. When Plowright had finished his speech, Gonzalez spoke again.

"And what have you got to say for yourself?"

"Eh?" Plowright asked, but Fargo knew the question was directed at him. He chose his words carefully.

"Just here to help Mr. Plowright," Fargo said. He shrugged diffidently, scuffled his feet, and wiped his hands nervously on his leather apron. Apparently, the ruse worked. Fargo sensed the padre relaxed slightly.

"I see." Gonzalez watched them for another moment, then half turned away. "But no one at the pueblo has need of your services. You may go."

"We got those wagon wheel rims," one of the monks put in, his voice a low growl like gravel in an empty bucket. "You know. Those four wagons. They need some work."

The hooded priest nodded.

"Thank you, Brother Emilio," he said. "You are right. Well, Mr. Plowright, you and your assistant have arrived just in time after all. Maybe as the answer to our prayers. You may remain only until the work is completed on these wagons. But I warn you that the Lord God has wrought many changes here at Black Mesa. The Lord God has a divine purpose for this flock, and He has gathered them all into the fold. Now, if you are to stay, you must promise to abide by our rules."

"Sure," Plowright agreed hastily. "Sure, padre."

Fargo was about to ask just what these rules were when there was a disturbance at the back of the chapel. They turned to see a Tewa woman being dragged forward by the skinny Tewa man Fargo had seen in Santa Fe. Her hair was wild and obscured her face. She was dressed in ragged clothes and struggling in his grasp, trying to wrench herself free.

Instinctively, Fargo moved forward and seized the skinny man by the arm, pulling him away from the woman. The woman ducked and then cowered behind Fargo. The skinny man reacted instantaneously, drawing his gun.

"What . . . what?" the skinny man stuttered, waving the barrel of his pistol wildly in Fargo's direction. He seemed out of control, nervous, as if he would shoot at any second.

"Broken Stick!" Robin Plowright exclaimed. At the sound of the name, the skinny man glared at the smithy and the woman looked up in surprise. "I thought you were banished from Black Mesa," Plowright said wonderingly. "What are you doing here?"

"Why if it isn't old Plowright the blacksmith," the skinny Tewa snarled. "My name's Fraco now. And see, I'm helping the monks here. I found God.

Thanks to Padre Gonzalez. So the tribe took me back. I'm an important man now, Plowright."

"Well," Plowright said, obviously taken aback momentarily. "Well, ain't that a lucky thing?"

Fraco waved his pistol at Fargo to stand aside. The woman hunched down behind him. Fargo hesitated, unwilling to let her be mistreated again.

"Mr. Foster," the padre's voice boomed. For a moment Fargo didn't realize Gonzalez was speaking to him. Then he turned about. "Mr. Foster, step aside. Please do not interfere in what does not concern you."

"Ha!" the woman muttered under her breath. She swung her face toward them, and her tangled hair parted so that Fargo glimpsed her face. She was a striking woman of about thirty, although her cheeks were streaked with dirt. Fargo heard Plowright gasp, then the old man coughed as if to cover the sound. "Ha!" she said again defiantly.

Fargo considered disobeying the padre's order. He was reluctant to give the woman over to the gun-toting and cruel Fraco. But, he realized, he was badly outnumbered and without his Colt. There was nothing he could do. Not at the moment. And he had to play the role of blacksmith's assistant. He shrugged and moved aside.

Fraco pulled the woman roughly toward him and drew back his arm as if to hit her. A flicker of movement from the padre stopped him. Fraco let his arm drop.

"I see there is a matter of faith that we must deal with," Gonzalez said. His voice was as heavy as

71

honey, his words resonant in the barrel vault of the chapel. He waved a dismissive hand at Fargo and Plowright.

"Brother Juan and Brother Emilio will show you where you may work. They will explain the rules. You may stay one night only. Then you must leave us."

The two monks came up on either side and escorted them from the chapel. As they were leaving, Fargo heard the woman cry out. He turned back, but the big monk named Juan blocked his way. Once outside in the hot sun, Juan and Emilio directed them to bring their wagon around toward an open shed that faced the main plaza.

"Here is where you work," Juan said curtly, gesturing toward the shed that had a smoke hole in the ramshackle roof and a firepit surrounded by stones. "We will bring the wagons that need repair."

"And what about those rules Gonzalez was talking about?" Fargo asked.

"For the protection of the pueblo," Juan said, "all visitors must be locked into the guest quarters at sunset. You will be freed again at dawn."

"What the hell?" Fargo said. "Locked up for the night?"

"The padre's orders," Juan said.

As soon as the two monks left, Fargo and Plowright set to unpacking.

"Things sure have changed around here," Plowright muttered, lifting bars of pig iron out of the wagon. "And for the worse."

"Who was that woman?" Fargo grunted as he carried the big anvil into the shed. He thought of the lithe woman struggling in Fraco's grasp, her hair wild around her face.

Plowright scowled at the question.

"That was Ernesta. Her Tewa name's Dawn Mountain. She's Lucero's daughter. Used to be a beautiful woman. She looked like hell."

"Or like she'd been through hell," Fargo said.

Ernesta had obviously been mistreated by Fraco—and probably Padre Gonzalez, too. She seemed like the rebellious sort. Whatever was going on here, he was sure Ernesta would tell him if he could just get close enough or get her alone to talk to her.

"And who's this Fraco character?" Fargo asked. He had to repeat the question in a loud voice before Plowright understood.

"His real name's Broken Stick," the smithy said as they began stacking a load of wood neatly beside the firepit. "And he's trouble. He was born trouble. Even as a boy Broken Stick was stealing from his own people, always getting into fights and causing a ruckus. Finally, when he was sixteen, he killed another Tewa boy. So the tribe threw him out. Sent him into exile and he just disappeared. That was four years ago. I'm surprised to see him back here, but I guess he got himself religion and that makes everything all right."

"He doesn't look too holy to me," Fargo muttered, remembering the skinny man's beady eyes and narrow face.

They looked up to see Emilio and Juan driving the first of the wagons toward them. It was not an ordinary freight wagon as Fargo had imagined, but a tall enclosed wagon with one barred window over the driver's seat.

"Why, that looks like a wagon for transporting prisoners," Plowright said. "What do you think—" Fargo shushed him as the men pulled up the wagon and clambered down. Emilio unhitched the two burros from the traces and led them away. While Juan and Plowright watched, Fargo made a great show of inspecting the wagon's underside. A glance told him that the wagon needed only minor repair on the worn iron wheel rims and cracked wheel blocks.

"Somebody's tried to repair this already," Plowright said, running his finger over an unsuccessful flaking patch on one of the wheel rims.

"Yeah," Emilio said in his gravelly voice. "Just get to work on it. And you're not supposed to wander around. Stay right here. That's what the padre said."

Plowright and Fargo got down to work. As they removed the wheel from the first of the prison wagons, Fargo kept an eye out. He caught sight of Emilio lurking on one side of the plaza, clearly keeping watch on them. For the next few hours, as they melted the iron and forged new wheel rims, there were hardly any Tewa to be seen on the dusty streets.

"Sure is strange around here," Plowright said over the whistling of the bellows and the ring of the beaten metal on the anvil. "In the old days this pueblo used to be bustling with activity. And now? It's like a graveyard."

Smithing was hot work. The fire was blasting. Hour by hour, they heated the metal, red hot, then white hot. They poured it into molds to make new pins for the worn blocks and beat it into new rims for the wheels. The heat rose in waves and their sweat fell and hissed on the coals.

As the red sun lowered alongside the tall side of Black Mesa, Emilio and Juan appeared. Plowright and Fargo had just about finished work on the second wagon.

"Time to go to your quarters," Juan said.

"Eh?" Plowright said, looking up from hammering on the iron. "Oh, yeah. Hold on a minute. We just got a little more on this one rim."

"I said now," Juan said loudly. Emilio kicked some dirt into the fire, getting some into the crucible where the iron was red hot.

"Hey," Plowright protested. Fargo realized there was no point in resisting. That would only raise suspicions. He doused the fire, and the smithy brought their gear from the wagon. On the way to the guest quarters they stopped off at the shed where the Ovaro and Plowright's nag were stabled. Fargo made sure the pinto had sufficient oats and water before they left.

They emerged from the stable as the red light washed over the adobe dwellings. Fargo was just starting to wonder if there were any Tewa at all in the pueblo when the Indians began to emerge from the doors. Like the Tewa he had seen in Santa Fe, the men, women, and children seemed as dazed as sleepwalkers. They seemed not to even notice him and Plowright as they came out and began walking toward the central plaza. More and more appeared in the dusty street, all heading the same direction.

"Hey, there's old Wing-Wind," Plowright said, waving at an Indian coming toward them, walking dazedly. The smithy suddenly broke away and grabbed the arm of the Tewa who looked at him blankly. "It's me, Plowright," the smithy yelled in the Indian's face. He shook his arm. For an instant the Tewa's face flickered with recognition, but then Emilio and Juan closed in.

"That's enough," Juan snapped, jerking Plowright away. Emilio pushed the Tewa back into the swarm of Indians making their way toward the plaza.

"But Wing-Wind's an old friend of mine," Plowright said.

"The rules of the pueblo," Juan said. "The Tewa want to be left in peace. They do not want strangers interfering."

"The hell you say," Plowright muttered under his breath.

"What's going on anyway?" Fargo asked Juan. "Where are they all going? To some kind of meeting?"

Juan ignored the question.

"This is where you're staying for the night," he said, opening a wide wooden door. "Food will come later." Without another word he shoved them inside and slammed the door behind them. Fargo glanced around as he heard the sound of a key grating in the lock.

Now they were prisoners. The last of the ruddy light filtered in through one small barred window. The adobe interior was spacious and whitewashed with two rope beds and several rough tables and chairs. Some wood was stacked beside a stone fireplace. Jugs of water and a basin stood nearby.

"Well," Plowright said, glancing back at the locked door. "This sure ain't like the old days. But at least let's get washed up."

While the old smithy was splashing in the basin, Fargo tried the lock on the door. It was new, cast of solid iron, impossible to break from the inside. He tried all the bars at the window, but they too were immovable. Short of a stick of dynamite, he thought, it would be impossible to break out of here. Fargo found some oil lamps and lit them as the last of the light faded from the room. Hell, he hated to be trapped, locked in. What was going on out there anyway? As if divining his thoughts, Plowright spoke.

"Those Tewa looked damn strange," the smithy said as he was toweling off. "And Wind-Wing. Hell, he can't have forgotten me. And I saw some others I knew, too. Not one of them even looked at us. There's something wrong with them all, I tell you."

"I think so, too," said Fargo. He had to repeat himself so the smithy could hear him. "But we sure can't find out anything locked up in here. We've got to get out."

He angrily paced the floor and tried the door again. Even the ceiling was solid, timbered with heavy beams. A sound came from the door, and he heard Juan shout that he was bringing in their supper. Fargo had a sudden idea. He grabbed a poker from the fireplace and hastened toward the door, gesturing for Plowright to follow. Fargo positioned himself behind the door as it swung open. If he jumped the monk while the door was open, they could slip out for a while and figure out what was going on out there. Fargo raised the poker, ready to bring it down on the monk's head as he passed by.

"Well, you brought six of your friends," Plowright said loudly as he stood in the doorway. It was a signal and Fargo knew it. They were outnumbered, and any attempt to escape would just blow their whole plan. Fargo lowered the poker and rested it against the wall as Juan passed by carrying a tray of covered dishes. Fargo stepped out from behind the door and Juan started to see him there. The monk put down the food and left without a word. The door closed again.

"You think they were suspecting we'd try something?" Plowright asked.

"I don't know," Fargo said. As the smithy dished the food out into bowls, Fargo angrily pulled at the barred window again. And he heard a sound, the low scrape of someone against the rough exterior of the adobe. There was someone standing outside listening. He'd probably been listening since they'd been locked in. And, with the old man's deafness, they'd been talking pretty loudly. Whoever it was had heard every word. Fargo tried to remember what they had said. As far as he could recall, it was enough to let their captors know that they were troublemakers, but not enough to reveal the real reason for being there.

Fargo returned to the table where Plowright was setting down bowls of steaming beans and a basket of tortillas. It was impossible for the old man to hear a whisper. So, using gestures, Fargo mimed that there was someone outside listening. The smithy looked confused for a moment, then he got the message and nodded thoughtfully.

"Good food," Fargo said loudly as they began to eat.

"I guess when this job is done, we won't come back this way," Plowright said. Fargo nodded at the direction of the conversation. Whoever was listening needed to get the message that they were just blacksmithing. "I sure don't like the hospitality here. And I think these Black Mesa Indians are just getting too crazy."

"Yeah, I never did like Indians," Fargo said for the benefit of the eavesdropper. "I'd rather be doing work up in Denver City."

"I guess you're right," Plowright agreed. "Let's get this job done as quick as we can and then get the hell out of here."

"Suits me," Fargo said.

They continued to make small talk as they finished their meal, and then Plowright made his way to the fireplace where he had laid a pile of wood and pulled out his tinder box. Just as he was about to light it, Fargo rushed to his side and held back his hand. He poked his head into the fireplace and looked up. The chimney was wide and squat. Large enough to climb through with hand and foot holds in the rough rock. At the top of the black tunnel, he could see a rectangular patch of stars in the clear night sky.

Fargo sat back on his heels as his plan took shape. Yes, he could make his way up the chimney fairly easily. Only problem was, it would make some noise, and whoever was keeping watch over them was going to hear him. The old smithy seemed to follow his thoughts and his wrinkled face took on a look of worry. All at once he brightened, went to his saddlebag, and pulled out his harmonica and his tambourine with the foot pedal.

"I got a good idea of how we'll pass the time," Plowright said in a loud voice. "You play this tambourine here, and I'll blow some tunes on this harmonica."

"Good idea," Fargo said with a wink. Whoever was listening would assume that there were two people inside making music. The music would cover up the sound of Fargo's escape up the chimney, and the smithy could keep up the ruse for hours, giving Fargo plenty of time to scout out the pueblo. Plowright took a seat just to one side of the barred window and set up the tambourine with the pedal on the wooden floor.

"No, you're not getting it quite right," Plowright admonished, as if he were speaking to Fargo as he beat an awkward rhythm on the tambourine. "There, that's better," the smithy said. He began playing "O, Susanna" on his mouth organ. It was painfully out of tune.

As the strains of the music filled the air, Fargo pushed aside the pile of wood and pulled himself up into the chimney. Wood smoke stung his nose. He reached for the first handhold and found a projecting rock, slick with old soot. He pulled himself upward, hand over hand, ascending the chimney. His toe missed a foothold, and his boot scraped loudly against the rough rock. He paused, waited and listened, but could hear nothing except the raucous sound of Plowright's music. As he neared the top of the chimney, he caught a whiff of the cold air of the desert night. He came up warily, listening, watching. If the man standing guard had heard any noise from inside the chimney, he might be standing down below ready to blow Fargo's head off as he came out. Just to be on the safe side, Fargo unknotted his neckerchief and waved it in the open air. Nothing happened. No shout. No gunshot.

Fargo slowly raised his head above the top of the chimney and scanned the area. The flat roof stretched away before him. The night was starlit, with moonrise still an hour away. His keen eyes sought the darkness around the adobe house, but there was nothing to be seen. The roofline hid whoever was keeping watch underneath the barred window. And there was no one else in sight.

Fargo pulled himself silently out of the chimney and hunched down beside it for a moment. He glanced toward the plaza, but other buildings obscured his view. To the west the huge hulk of Black Mesa rose in the sky, obliterating the stars.

Knees bent, Fargo silently ran across the roof toward the back, opposite the barred window. With the agility of a cat, he let himself down over the side, dangling for an instant from the roofline, then dropping with a thud onto the ground. A dog began barking nearby. Fargo shrank back against the wall into a shadow as he heard the sound of someone coming. In a moment a figure appeared around the corner of the building and stood for a moment. The dog barked a few more times and then quieted. The waiting figure disappeared again. A close call.

The only thing that could ruin their plan was if the guard got suspicious enough to open up the door and look in. Then he would find the old smithy alone. Well, he couldn't worry about that possibility now. Fargo made his way silently along the side of the building to the narrow street until he could ease around the corner. There he spotted the dark figure standing under the barred window as the strains of music wafted out into the night air. The man moved restlessly, and Fargo recognized Emilio. Keeping the corner of the house between him and the guard, Fargo backed away, down the dark and empty street. Then he turned and made his way quietly through the pueblo toward the main plaza.

When he reached the open area, it was deserted. He had seen no one, heard no one. He spotted a light shining through the colored glass windows in the chapel. Maybe they were all inside having a service. He dashed across the plaza and came up to the chapel. No sound. He eased open the huge wooden door a crack and peered inside. The space was deserted, and a single candle burned on the altar. Fargo slipped inside.

The vaulted ceiling echoed every tiny sound as he made his way down the aisle between the empty benches. A small door stood on one side of the dais. It was locked. Fargo looked through the keyhole, but could see only blackness. What was behind the door?

He cursed and tried the door again. The lock was an old one, he saw. Swiftly, he pulled the knife from the scabbard strapped to his ankle and wedged the point between the door and the jamb. He jiggled it back and forth at the same time, forcing the handle of the door upward. In a moment he felt the point of the knife slide further and the bolt slid backward. The door eased open with a groan. Fargo took one of the small candles nearby, lit it, and entered.

The room was long and narrow—clearly Padre Gonzalez's inner sanctum. Several tables stood along the wall on which were piled documents, various bottles of ink, and feather quills. At another end stood a wooden rack with dozens of glass vials, bottles, and canisters full of herbs and powders. Obviously medicines, Fargo thought, wondering why the padre would need so many medical supplies. Nearby, a gun rack, stacked with rifles, hung on the wall.

Fargo made his way to the desk and picked up the first of the documents. It seemed to be the second page of a letter, written on thick parchment with heavy flourishes. He scanned it quickly—something about the establishment of a new mission in Mexico and how everyone in the Church must make sacrifices to help the new mission succeed. The letter was unfinished, unsigned.

Just then he heard the sound of several men entering the chapel. The sounds of their voices and the heavy tread of their boots on the stone floor echoed through the empty space. Fargo swore to himself, realizing they would see the small door open beside the altar and notice the flickering of his candle. And if they caught him in here, the whole game was up. He would never find out what in hell was going on and who had killed Lucero and why.

"Who's there?" a voice suddenly boomed.

Fargo looked around the room. There was no place to hide—no corners—and no gun in his hand. He cursed silently.

"I said, who's there?" the voice asked again. Unmistakable. The voice belonged to Padre Claudio Gonzalez.

4

Fargo looked around for a place to hide, but there was no cover. He made a quick grab for a monk's robe hanging on the row of pegs and pulled it on over his head. He had just finished tying the rope belt around his waist and pulling the hood over his head when a figure in black strode into the room. Padre Gonzalez. Fargo turned away to hide his face.

"What are you doing in here?" the padre said.

"Trigger jammed," Fargo said, mimicking Emilio's gravelly voice. "Need a better rifle."

Fargo made his way to the gun rack and pretended to peruse the firearms. Suddenly, he spotted his own Henry and took it. It was good to have the trusty rifle in his hands again. His trusty Colt was nowhere to be seen.

"You're supposed to be guarding our visitors, Emilio," Gonzalez said sharply. "Don't leave your post again." Fargo nodded, keeping his face averted. For a moment he considered a shootout with Gonzalez and the monks, but he still didn't know what their game was. He could feel the padre's suspicions as he stood expectantly in the darkened room.

"How did you get in here?" Gonzalez suddenly asked.

"Door was open," Fargo rasped in Emilio's tone of voice. The padre nodded, seeming to accept the explanation.

"Hey, Gonzalez," one of the monks called out as he entered the room. The voice was Juan's. "We got 'em all up on the mesa. And it's time for a showdown with the girl."

"That's right," Fraco said with a nervous laugh. "Time for the tribe to pay for what they did to me."

The padre crossed to the table stacked with documents. He reached for one rolled up and tied with a large red ribbon.

"Here it is," he said as Fraco came up to the table. "Your payment."

"As soon as you get all those elders to sign it," Fraco said.

"Oh, they'll sign," Gonzalez said. With a lightning fast movement, the priest suddenly reached out and grabbed the front of Fraco's shirt, pulling him close. The skinny man struggled nervously in Gonzalez's grip. The hooded priest, his face lost in dark shadows, held the man for a long moment, then released him. "Just don't try to double-cross me," Gonzalez growled.

"I won't," Fraco said in a high voice. "I got what I want. You'll get your payments. Regular like. Soon as the land agent starts making the sales."

Fargo wondered what was going on. It was clear Gonzalez was no priest. But then, who was he? Fargo suddenly felt Gonzalez's stare on him, and he left the room, pushing through the other huddled monks standing just outside in the chapel. Although he was curious, he didn't dare risk hanging around to hear more. He left the chapel hurriedly, hoping no one would stop to talk with him. He slipped out of the door and hastened to one side of the chapel, secreting himself in the shadow by the corner. A moment later, the group exited and set off across the plaza.

Fargo waited until they were nearly out of sight and then followed them, gathering the robe around him and sprinting from building to building as they made their way to the edge of the pueblo, heading in the direction of Black Mesa. Padre Gonzalez and his men mounted burros waiting at the bottom of the trail and started climbing the switchback trail that led up the steep side of the mammoth butte. Following them without being seen was difficult, since the trail wound back and forth. They only had to glance down to see him, so Fargo waited in the shadow of a rocky cliff until they were barely visible, far up on the trail. Then he began climbing with the rifle slung over his shoulder. The robe made climbing more difficult, so he hitched it up with the rope belt. There was no need to take it off. It might come in handy.

His eyes adjusted to the starlight and the dim plain and the pueblo dwellings as they fell away below him. Higher and higher he went, over the rocky trail. A half hour later, he was nearly to the top. He slowed, moving warily, keeping an eye on the trail above. If they had a lookout posted at the top of the trail, Fargo knew he was sure to be seen. He scanned the steep rock for another way up and finally spotted a slope of boulders next to the trail. He left the switchbacks and climbed for another ten minutes, over and under the huge rocks as he made his way silently to the crest of the butte. The dark land was far below, and a glow above the mountains to the east showed where the moon would soon rise.

He climbed up a precipitous gully between huge rocks and glanced up to see the open sky above him, filled with stars. He was there. He slowly eased himself upward, inch by inch, until he could see over the last rocks and across the top of Black Mesa.

Just then the moon pushed upward and light spilled across the landscape. Nearby, he saw low rock cairns and poles with tatters of feathers and ragged cloth blowing in the night wind. A Tewa burial ground, a holy place for the tribe.

Some distance away, across the wide rocky expanse of the mesa top, he spotted a strange adobe building. It seemed to be circular and open to the sky. He could see light coming from the top of it and hear voices, but he was too far away to make out what was being said. To one side were the burros that the padre and his men had ridden. A couple of dark figures could be seen walking back and forth. Fargo took a quick glance around and sprinted across the rugged terrain, pausing from time to time to look around as he made his way toward the strange building.

As he got closer and the moon rose higher, he saw that there were two monks walking back and forth in front of the enclosure and a third figure that did not move at all. As Fargo came nearer, he saw it was a woman. She stood, chained by the wrists and ankles between two upright poles, her arms and legs pulled wide apart. He hunched behind a rock for a long time watching until he finally recognized Ernesta. The day before she had looked like a wild woman, her hair and dress ragged and disheveled. But tonight her hair was arranged in the two buns the Tewa women wore over their ears, and she was wearing turquoise jewelry and a cotton dress.

Fraco appeared around one side of the building, heading toward Ernesta. In his hand he carried a long bullwhip, and a ring of keys jangled at his belt. He slowly approached Ernesta and chucked her under the chin. She spat in his face. Fraco swore and stepped backward. The other two monks went inside. Fargo crept up behind some rocks, close enough so that he could hear what they were saying.

"Think you're so high and mighty, Dawn Mountain," Fraco said, using her Tewa name and speaking in Tanoan, the language of the tribe. Fargo knew the language since it was similar to what the Kiowa spoke. Fraco wound the whip around one hand, then cracked it in the air. "Oh, yes, I've waited a long time for this," Fraco said. "I've waited a long time to make you pay."

"Broken Stick sounds like a white man," Ernesta said defiantly. "Broken Stick is trying to be a big man, but he is still weak. He will never be—"

"Silence!" Fraco said. He stepped forward and grasped the front of her dress, ripping it downward. Fargo saw her smooth dark skin glisten in the moonlight, one of her high round breasts exposed. Fraco raised the whip over his head again and cracked it in the air.

"How will that feel on that pretty skin of yours?" he said. "I wanted you all dressed up for the party, just like I remember you when I was growing up and you wouldn't—"

"You murderer. I will never—"

Fraco raised the whip again and struck her on her bare shoulder. She recoiled, but did not cry out. Even in the moonlight Fargo could see the streak of blood across her flesh.

"Oh, but you will. You see, by tomorrow night, you will be all mine. And there will be no one here to stop me. No one here to help you."

Fury rose in Fargo, but he held himself back for a moment. He must be cool-headed. Figure out the way to free her and to get away. He gripped the cold steel of the Henry. Fifteen rounds, he thought. Enough to get her free? Enough to hold off the rest of them inside that building? As he watched, he idly checked the chamber. The rifle was empty—no bullets. Fargo swore silently. Hell. He hadn't stopped to check the rifle or to get bullets back in the chapel. There had been no time with Padre Gonzalez's suspicious gaze fixed on him. And now the rifle was useless.

Fargo secreted the Henry in a pile of rocks and darted closer, toward the line of waiting burros. The long-eared beasts stood patiently tethered, and Fargo moved among them quietly, patting their flanks to keep them from being startled by his presence. He pulled the hood over his head again and low down over his face. He was only ten feet from Fraco, who had taken no notice of him. In another moment . . .

"You there!" a monk called out as three of them emerged from one side of the enclosure. "Get inside and help!" Fargo hesitated a moment, looking back toward Fraco and Ernesta.

Fargo realized the entrance to the building must be around the other side, so he headed in that direction and found the arched doorway with light spilling out of it. The sound of chanting filled the circular enclosure, and he heard something else as well—moaning, as if many of the Tewa were in pain. Fargo stood in the doorway and looked in at the odd gathering. Several of the monks were carrying torches, which threw a weird light over the scene. About a hundred and fifty Tewa—the whole tribe—stood swaying or sat on the ground, many of them holding their heads or stomachs. A line of Indians knelt at one end where Padre Gonzalez stood on a dais near a rude altar made of a rock slab.

"Take this up front," someone said, nudging his elbow. Fargo turned as one of the monks hastily passed him a plate of communion bread, small white pressed wafers. Fargo made his way through the crowd toward where Gonzalez was dispensing bread and wine to the Tewa.

"More," one of the Tewa whispered as he passed, grabbing onto his leg. "Give me more. Another one. Please."

Fargo stopped and gave one of the wafers to the Tewa who sat at his feet. The man's hands were shaking and his eyes had a hollow kind of desperation.

Other Tewa, seated around him looked up and raised their hands pleadingly, but he glanced over to see Gonzalez looking around for him. Fargo approached the priest, who was handing out the communion.

"Do you swear loyalty and obedience to the Church and to me as the shepherd of God's flock? Will you do whatever I command?" the padre was saying as a Tewa woman knelt before him to receive the wafer. She nodded eagerly as he gave her the bit of bread. The priest repeated the words to the next Tewa in line.

Fargo was no church-going man, but he knew damn well that the service was a fraud. Gonzalez was no priest. As he stood holding the plate of bread, his thoughts whirled. Padre Gonzalez was determined to completely control the whole tribe. But to what purpose? The tribe's chief, Lucero, had opposed Gonzalez and his monks. Lucero had figured out what they were up to. And they'd tortured and killed him for knowing. And now Lucero's daughter was rebelling, too. And she was chained up outside, probably awaiting the same fate as her father in the hands of the sadistic Fraco. But why weren't the rest of the Tewa up in arms? Why were they falling for this? Something was wrong with them, wrong with the whole show. Fargo watched as padre Gonzalez gave a bit of communion wafer to an old Tewa man with glassy eyes. Then Fargo realized. It was the wafers. Gonzalez and his men had put something in them to drug the Indians. That's what made them so complacent.

Fargo slid his hand across the plate and picked up

one of the wafers, hiding it inside the pocket of his shirt. He would examine it later.

"And now, let the elders come forth," Gonzalez's voice boomed. Several of the monks stepped forward to help six old Tewa men to their feet and up to the dais. Gonzalez pulled the red-ribboned document Fargo had seen before and unrolled it. He placed it on the rock slab altar and pulled out a bottle of ink and the quill. One by one, the old men bent over the document and, as if in a dream, made their marks on it. Gonzalez stood over them, watching. Fargo wondered what could possibly be written there. Fraco had said it was his payment, and then Gonzalez had warned him not to double-cross him. But how?

He noticed Fraco had come to the doorway and stood in the crowd of monks. He was rubbing his hands together in glee as he watched the signing of the document. The ring of keys at his belt glimmered in the dim light. Fargo saw his opportunity. He put down the tray of bread and made his way toward the group of monks. Just as he reached the doorway, Fargo pretended to stumble. He pitched forward, colliding with Fraco, who staggered backward into another man.

"Hey, watch it," Fargo growled at a monk standing nearby as if the man had tripped him.

"You watch it," Fraco snapped, regaining his feet. Fargo pushed his way out of the door to the darkness beyond. In his hand was the ring of keys from Fraco's belt.

Ernesta's head was hanging low as he approached, her dress ripped open to reveal her high round breasts. A dark streak on her shoulder showed where Fraco's whip had bit her. As he approached, she looked up.

"Come back for more?" she said defiantly, mistaking him for Fraco.

"Quiet. I've come to help," he said in a low voice as he tried one of the keys in the padlock at her wrist. It didn't fit, but the second one did and the lock sprang open. Ernesta withdrew her arm as he began unlocking the other.

"Who are you?" she whispered, wonderingly. As he freed her other wrist, he glanced up at her, his hood fell back, and the moonlight struck his face. "You're that blacksmith—Plowright's assistant!" she said, puzzlement in her voice. She rubbed her wrists as he knelt down to free her ankles.

"My real name's Skye Fargo," he said. He heard her sharp intake of breath. She recognized his name. One foot was free. He moved to the last padlock, which was rusted. Suddenly, he heard the sounds of someone approaching around the side of the enclosure. The key wouldn't turn. Ernesta tugged, frustrated, on the chain that still held her bound. No time. In another moment Fargo pulled up his hood and wordlessly pulled her arm back toward the padlock. She understood and positioned herself so that it looked as if she were still chained.

Fargo had hoped it was Fraco. What he wouldn't give to have his hands around the skinny sadist's neck. But instead, it was one of the monks.

"Hey, you! What are you doing with that prisoner?"

"Checking out the padlocks," Fargo growled, using Emilio's voice again.

"Well, okay. Help me get the burros untied," the monk said shortly. Fargo nodded and followed the man a few short steps, then stooped and picked up a rock. His movement made the monk turn about just as Fargo raised his powerful arm and swung, catching the monk with a thud across the side of his skull. The monk swayed for an instant, and then his knees buckled and he fell. Fargo searched him, but the monk had no gun, no bullets. He dragged the inert body behind some rocks by the burros. He returned to Ernesta.

"Close call," he said, struggling to turn the key in the rusty lock. With a metallic rasp, the padlock sprang open. Ernesta made a sound like a small sob, and Fargo realized that, despite her defiant words to Fraco, she'd been deeply frightened.

"Let's get out of here," Fargo said. They could make better time running down the mountainside than riding on the burros. He grabbed the empty rifle from where he had hidden it, and they dashed across the rocky landscape. There was no time to lose. At any moment Ernesta's escape might be noticed, and Gonzalez and all his men would come after them. "What's going on here," Fargo asked as they raced down the trail.

"It's the priest, Gonzalez," Ernesta panted. "Ever since he came here, the whole pueblo's turned upside down."

"It's something in the communion bread, isn't it?" Fargo said.

"Exactly," Ernesta said. "From the first day my father and I refused to take communion from him. And then I pretended to, but I secretly hid it. There's something wrong with it. It makes everyone strange. Like ghosts."

"But why is Gonzalez doing it?" Fargo asked.

"He's trying to get the land. He says he had a vision from God that the Tewa should give the land to the Church." She paused to catch her breath as they stumbled down the rocky switchbacks.

"That must have been the document they were signing tonight," Fargo said. "The Tewa land grant?"

"Right," Ernesta said, her voice dispirited. "He talked the elders into signing it all over to Fraco. So, as of tomorrow, all this land belongs to him. Not to the tribe."

"Tomorrow?"

"That's when the white man's judge comes to Santa Fe," Ernesta said. "Gonzalez will take the document to him, and then the land will belong to Fraco. Fraco!" She spit at the name. "Broken Stick! If only my father would come back. He would take care of that murderer!"

"Your father? Wasn't your father Lucero?" Fargo asked.

"Yes," Ernesta said, hesitating, a strange note in her voice. "He never trusted Gonzalez. And a week ago he told me he had to go on a short trip. But he hasn't returned."

There was a moment of silence as Fargo considered his next words. They had nearly reached the bottom of Black Mesa. Suddenly Fargo heard voices shouting far above them. Ernesta's escape had been discovered. No time to tell her her father was dead. That would have to come later.

"We're going to ride into Santa Fe for help," Fargo said. "First we need horses. And we need to get Plowright." He couldn't leave the old smithy behind. Gonzalez would kill him for certain.

They ran through the deserted streets of the pueblo. But when the stable came into view, Fargo stopped short. He ducked down behind a low adobe wall and looked out.

Beside the stable stood the two box wagons that Fargo and Plowright had repaired that afternoon. Five monks stood uneasily nearby, their rifles gleaming in the moonlight. The sounds of pursuit—shouts and gunfire—could be heard from the direction of Black Mesa. The monks were on alert. Fargo swore under his breath. There was no way he could overpower five of them.

"What do we do now?" Ernesta whispered.

"No time to explain. Just get ready to follow me," Fargo said. He puckered his lips and whistled, a distinctive sound that carried for a long distance. The monks looked around, confused. Fargo repeated the sound and inside the stable, the Ovaro began battering the wooden door with its powerful hooves. The monks hesitated, then three of them went to the doors of the stable while the other two headed straight toward the sound of Fargo's whistle.

It was just as he hoped, Fargo thought as they dashed behind the low adobe wall and around a small building. He led Ernesta down a dark street and then turned back again. From the direction of the stable, he heard the whinny of the pinto. Fargo whistled again and heard men shouting, and then the sound of pounding hooves. Again he whistled and in another moment, the black-and-white pinto appeared at the end of the street, galloping straight toward them.

"Ride to Santa Fe," Fargo said as the horse stopped alongside them. He lifted her onto its bareback. "Find Padre Fernandez or the sheriff."

"Skye! Aren't you coming with me?"

"Go!" he said to her, slapping the pinto's flank. The Ovaro hesitated a moment, then sped off down the street. Fargo melted away into the shadows not a moment too soon. At the other end of the street a crowd of monks appeared. With his rifle in hand, Fargo sprinted toward the house where Robin Plowright was being held. Long before he got there, he heard the strains of the harmonica, way out of tune. The old smithy was still playing.

Fargo crept around the side of the building and peered over at where Emilio was standing guard. The man was sitting against the wall, fast asleep. The shouting came nearer. It would be only a matter of moments before the monks decided to check on their visitors. Moving fast, Fargo climbed onto the roof, left the Henry and the monk's robe beside the chimney, and let himself down into the flue. Never mind the noise he decided as his boots scraped against the rocks. The monks would arrive any minute. Fargo dropped the last few feet and crawled out of the fireplace. Plowright, still sitting beside the high-barred window, blowing tiredly on the harmonica and giving an occasional beat to the drum with his foot, raised his eyebrows but continued playing.

Fargo realized he was smeared with soot. He stripped off his jacket and balled it up, inside out. He grabbed a dark wool blanket from the bed and dashed water over it from the pitcher, then quickly rubbed his face and hands. It wasn't a great job, but in the low light he might get away with it. The shouting of men came from just outside now. Fargo threw himself down on the floor beside Plowright's chair. He had just disassembled the foot pedal, hid the pieces inside his shirt, and began to beat on tambourine, when Juan and Emilio burst through the door.

"Did you come for the concert?" Fargo asked pleasantly, shaking the tambourine.

Plowright launched into an energetic and barely recognizable rendition of "My Old Kentucky Home." Juan scowled. Fargo sang a few bars at the top of his lungs.

Just then, Padre Gonzalez stroke in.

"Silence! Silence!" Juan shouted.

"See?" Emilio growled. "I told you they both been in here all night, making this racket. "I heard one of 'em on that drum thing and the other one blowing that damn mouth organ. They been going for hours."

Padre Gonzalez, his face as always hidden in the shadow beneath his hood, slowly walked around the room, examining the beds and the table with the empty dishes where they had eaten dinner. The priest didn't spot Fargo's jacket, which he had jammed underneath his pillow. But he did stop for a long moment at the washstand where the white china pitcher had a big black handprint on it. He turned slowly and seemed to stare right through Fargo.

"No," he said at last as if to himself. "If you had escaped this place tonight, you would not have returned."

"Huh?" Fargo said, playing the role.

Gonzalez spun on his heels and left hurriedly.

"You want to play some more?" Plowright asked him loudly as the door was being shut behind the monks.

"Guess we ought to turn in," Fargo said. "Wonder what all that excitement was about?" He had no doubt that the monks were listening at the window again.

"Got me. Good night, then," Plowright said loudly.

Fargo put out the light, crept to the barred window, and stood on a chair to look out. Two men stood watch now. One stood beneath the window, and the other walked back and forth along the street. He doubted he could get away with escaping up the chimney again. But that didn't matter. Because Ernesta was on her way to Santa Fe.

As Fargo was undressing, he felt the wafer in his shirt pocket. He smelled it—a vaguely familiar odor like mushrooms. Curious, he bit off a small piece and chewed it. It didn't taste like much. He put the rest back into his pocket, and then he lay down to sleep.

Something woke him, the sound of something moving. Something huge, brushing against the floor. Fargo rolled over, reaching for his Colt. It was not there. His hand closed on nothingness, and then he saw it. Crawling across the floor, a huge snake, longer than a man, with glittering green scales and ruby eyes. Fargo sat up in bed. His rifle was on the roof, he vaguely remembered. The snake seemed to read his thoughts, and its head turned slowly, the ruby eyes glittering red in the darkness. Fargo told himself he was having a bad dream, but it seemed very real. The snake opened its mouth, and its fangs dripped poison. The forked tongue flicked in and out. Fargo gripped the edge of the bed. The snake was not real, he told himself again. It slid across the floor, closer, then raised itself until its head was level with Fargo's. The eyes were hypnotic, piercing. There was nothing he could do. His body was paralyzed, and a deep warmth suffused all his limbs. He just wanted to lie still and watch what the snake would do. He was helpless. No, Fargo told himself. With a great effort he reached out and grasped the snake with both hands. It fought back, squirming in his grip, as he held on.

"Fargo! Fargo!" the sound was strangled, distant.

His vision cleared, and he realized he was holding Plowright between his hands, shaking the old man back and forth. Fargo released him, and the smithy staggered backward.

"My God," the old man said, watching Fargo warily.

Fargo sat on the edge of the bed, holding his pounding head in his hands. His throat was dry. He stumbled toward the water pitcher and drank, then dashed the rest over his head.

"I'm all right now," he said to the smithy. He kept

his voice as low as he could, remembering that the guards might be listening.

"Some bad dream," Plowright said. "I thought you were going to kill me." Fargo pulled the wafer out of his shirt pocket.

"It's this," he explained, showing the communion bread to Plowright. The smithy shook his head wonderingly. "I'll tell you tomorrow."

There was no way for him to explain to Plowright without raising his voice. But the experience made Fargo realize how powerful the drugs were. He had taken only a small bite of the wafer, whereas the Tewa were eating a whole one, at least, every day. And it had made him feel powerless, lacking will. No wonder the whole Tewa tribe looked like sleepwalkers. Fargo suddenly remembered how Padre Fernandez had talked of his visit with Gonzalez and how he had taken communion and then had the vision of snakes that he had interpreted as his envy of his successful rival. And Gonzalez had even told the padre he would have a vision. But it had been the drug. Fargo lay awake the rest of the night, his thoughts on Gonzalez. Just before dawn he heard sounds, and he rose and stood at the barred window, listening. The noise was distant, but he thought he heard horses and shouting from the direction of the plaza. After a few minutes it died down again.

Restless, Fargo scrubbed the soot off his jacket and changed his Levi's. No need to give Gonzalez and his men any inkling of how he had escaped. Then he spent some time honing the blade of the knife strapped to his ankle. After one of the monks brought breakfast, they were ordered outside and led back to the shed to finish the work on the last two wagons. Today Juan and Emilio and four monks guarded them, all with rifles. And once they lit the fire and got work underway, the monks remained, standing at various posts around the plaza, keeping an eye on them. Ernesta's mysterious escape had obviously put Gonzalez on his guard.

The first two wagons had been finished the day before and had been wheeled away. Fargo had seen them parked over by the stables. Plowright looked over the next two wagons they had to fix.

"Three busted wheel rims and a bad brake," he said. "Let's get going."

Fargo fed the fire while Plowright worked the bellows. Soon they had red-hot embers burning, and the smithy had melted enough iron to patch the rims and fashion a new joint for the brake block. They set to work, pouring the red-hot metal, holding the cooling pieces with tongs, and beating the metal with blows from the heavy hammer. All the time Fargo kept his eye on the plaza and the movement of the monks.

At midmorning the door to the chapel opened and Padre Gonzalez stepped outside, along with Fraco and the six elderly Tewa men Fargo had seen sign the land grant the night before. Gonzalez carried several documents under his arm. They were going to meet the circuit judge in Santa Fe. And then all the land would belong to Fraco. A monk brought around a wagon, and they all got in and drove away. Fargo felt a sense of helpless rage as they rode out of sight. There was nothing he could do against all of Gonzalez's monks. And as for the land grant, maybe the judge would reverse his decision once he understood what had really happened.

As the sun crept toward noon, Fargo wondered where Ernesta was. The sheriff and his men were bound to arrive any minute. Probably they had met up with the padre and his men on the road to Santa Fe and had taken them first.

Fargo was just fitting a new rim on a wagon wheel when he heard the pounding of hooves. Juan and Emilio started forward nervously, their rifles raised. Fargo grabbed an iron from the fire, as did Plowright. At least if it came down to a fight, they would be armed.

Three horsed riders galloped onto the plaza, raising a cloud of dust. When it cleared, Fargo saw two monks. The other figure was tall and dressed all in black. He rode a chestnut. Fargo stepped behind the wagon and peered out, watching what would happen.

"He was trying to enter the reservation," one of the monks said, his voice carrying clearly.

"What do you want?" Juan asked the stranger.

"I'm looking for somebody," the man said. "Somebody by the name of Skye Fargo."

"Skye Fargo?" Juan said thoughtfully. "I know that name. What do you want with him?"

"That's my business," the stranger growled.

"Nobody here by that name," Juan said shortly. "Now get off this land." The monks raised their rifles threateningly.

"Hold on a minute," the stranger said. "Maybe you've seen him around. Tall fellow, black beard, strong." Fargo saw Juan and several of the monks glance toward the shed.

"A lot of men look like that," Juan said.

"Well, then," the stranger said thoughtfully, "he rides a real distinctive horse. A pinto, black-and-white."

Juan nodded and several of the monks looked toward the shed again. From where they stood, they could see Plowright busying himself at his work but Fargo was out of sight.

Juan signaled to one of the monks who ran off and returned in a minute leading Fargo's Ovaro. Fargo felt stunned. What was the Ovaro doing back at Black Mesa? The horse was balking, resisting anyone's lead but Fargo's. The stranger, still sitting on his horse, took a long look around the pueblo and then glanced at the Ovaro.

"Is this Skye Fargo's horse?" Juan asked.

The stranger paused a moment, then shook his head.

"No. I know Fargo's horse and this ain't it. The markings are all wrong." He glanced around one more time, then touched his hand to his hat brim. "Guess I was mistaken. Somebody told me he was with the Tewa but, come to think of it, maybe they said Navajo."

"Take him back to the boundary," Juan said. The two monks rode off with the stranger. Fargo knelt down beside the wagon, pretending to adjust the brake, his thoughts whirling. If the Ovaro were here, then were was Ernesta? And who was the mysterious man in black?

Emilio passed by, leading the Ovaro back to the stable. Fargo got to his feet.

"Hey," Fargo said with a disarming smile. "You taking my horse out for a little walk?" The monk glared at Fargo, and the Ovaro nickered. Fargo walked over, patted its flank, and fell into step with Emilio. "Needs a little currying."

"Nice horse," Emilio said. The monk patted the Ovaro's nose.

Fargo glanced around behind him, but the monks on guard seemed to be taking no notice of him as he walked along with Emilio.

"Gonzalez makes everybody guard the road," Emilio said. "So that's how we caught the horse thief. The one who tried to steal your horse last night."

"Really?" Fargo said. They had left the plaza and were walking toward the stable. Obviously they had captured Ernesta. "You catch him?"

"Oh yeah," Emilio said. He smiled, obviously thinking he was outsmarting Fargo. "Locked *him* up." He chuckled and darted a quick glance toward the box wagons that stood beside the stable. Fargo cursed silently. So, they had intercepted Ernesta. And now they had her in one of the wagons. No help would come from Santa Fe.

"You boys are real smart," Fargo said. Emilio smiled broadly.

"Yeah. Gonzalez—he's real smart." Emilio opened the door to the stable, and for a moment Fargo considered overpowering him and riding out. But just then two monks appeared with their rifles. He would never escape alive. Fargo turned away.

"Guess I'll be getting back to work," he said. The two monks passed by, hardly looking at him. Fargo walked back, passing by the box wagons. He glanced around, but Emilio and the two monks had disappeared inside the stable. He knocked on the wooden side of the wagon, listened, but heard nothing. He moved to the second one and knocked on its padlocked door. Through the small barred window, he heard a rustling and then a creak as someone moved.

"It's me," he said in a low voice.

"Skye?" It was Ernesta. Her face appeared at the window. "They caught me, Skye. Ambushed me before I got off Tewa land. Oh, Skye, I don't know what we're going to do."

Fargo felt the presence of someone standing nearby before he even heard a sound.

"Oh, Skye," a male voice said. He turned slowly around and stared down the long barrel of a rifle. Juan's eyes glittered. "Oh, Skye Fargo," he said again, mimicking Ernesta. "I don't know what we're going to do."

5

Fargo knew there was no protesting the barrel of a rifle pointed straight at your chest.

Juan smiled a slow smile. "So, you're the famous Skye Fargo," he said. Fargo nodded, measuring the distance between them. With a sudden lunge he stepped sideways. Juan grunted and started to bring his rifle about, but Fargo advanced on him and grabbed the barrel as it swung around. Juan fired, and the bullet thudded harmlessly into the side of the other wagon.

Fargo hit Juan with his full weight, knocking the big man down. He kept a grip on the rifle barrel, trying to wrench it from the monk's grasp. Juan tried to point it toward him. He fired again, and the bullet flew wide into the sky.

"Hold it," a voice said. Fargo heard the click of a rifle off to his right and then another to his left. He glanced up to see three monks had converged on them, all with rifles pointed straight at him. It was hopeless, unless he wanted to be a dead man. Fargo let go of the rifle barrel.

Juan got to his feet, his face black with anger. He

beat the dust from his robe and jerked his head toward the wagon that held Ernesta.

"Let Mr. Skye Fargo cool off in there awhile," he snapped. "At least until Gonzalez gets back. Then we'll have some fun."

The wagon was unlocked, and Fargo was shoved inside. He had a glimpse of the bare interior of the wooden wagon and Ernesta's frightened face. Then the door slammed shut behind him. The monks laughed, and he heard their retreating footsteps.

There was a rustle of movement beside him as his eyes adjusted to the dimness. A little light filtered in through the small window in the door. He saw Ernesta's face, seeming to float in the darkness. He reached out and touched her arm. She shuddered and then she came to him, and he put his arm around her.

"I'm so frightened," she said. "Fraco and Gonzalez will kill us. I am sure of that."

"Not if I can help it," Fargo said. He rose and felt his way around the inside of the wagon, inspecting the wooden floor and the walls with his fingertips, which saw better in the near dark than his eyes. Nothing. Not a chink. No trap door. Not even a weak spot. He tried the ceiling, which was low enough for him to reach with outstretched arms. Nothing there either. Finally, he tried the window and the door. The bars were solid and the door fit tight. Even the hinges of the door were on the outside. There was no doubt the wagon had been designed to transport prisoners. There was no escape.

Nevertheless, Fargo pulled the knife from his

ankle scabbard. He slid the blade along the doorjamb until he encountered the bolt. For half an hour he worked, trying again and again to jimmy the lock, pushing until he feared snapping the point of the blade. But it was useless. The lock was solid.

"Well, I guess we just wait," Fargo said at last. He sat down and leaned against the wall. Ernesta sat close beside him. He could smell her odor, like sage and wood smoke. "Tell me how this all got started."

"Gonzalez came up to Black Mesa three months ago," Ernesta said. "We never had a priest here. We always traveled down to Chimayò."

"To Padre Fernandez."

"Yes," Ernesta said. He could feel her arm crossing herself in the dark. "Gonzalez came with a letter from the Pope—the chief priest in Rome—saying God had appointed Gonzalez to lead us. Everyone was very impressed. And, at first, so was I. So was my father." Fargo let the remark pass. Time to tell her about her father later. "And he brought Broken Stick with him, only now he was called Fraco."

"The Tewa had banished him, right?"

"That's right," she said. "Broken Stick had always been a troublemaker. And he always was after me. When he got older, one of the other boys made him jealous. And he murdered him. So my father told him he was disowned by the tribe."

"And then he showed up with Gonzalez."

"Every day at sunset Father Gonzalez gave the communion in the plaza. He was a man of thunder speech. And every day, I took the bread and wine.

And I began to feel . . . not myself. Different somehow."

"The drugs in the bread," Fargo said.

"Bad medicine," Ernesta said. "One day I was sick, and I stayed away and then I felt better. And the next day I started to hide the communion bread. I didn't eat it like the others."

"What about your father?"

"He refused from the very beginning. He believes the old Tewa gods are better. And he became more and more worried. A week ago something happened, and he said he was going away on a trip." There was a long pause. "He's dead, isn't he?" Ernesta said suddenly.

"Yes," Fargo answered her. He told her about how he had been with Lucero when he died. And about the message of the ring and the knotted rope he had left for Padre Fernandez. "The rope was knotted four times. And that was four days ago. I guess he meant something important was going to happen today."

"The document going to the judge in Santa Fe," Ernesta said.

"And he handed me some earth just before he died," Fargo remembered. "He was probably trying to say that Gonzalez was after the Tewa land."

"After Father disappeared," Ernesta remembered, her voice choked, "Gonzalez kept me under guard. And Gonzalez made some kind of deal with Fraco, that he would get all the Tewa land."

"In exchange for what, I wonder?" Fargo asked.

"I don't know," Ernesta said, troubled. "As long as the Tewa are alive, they will never leave Black Mesa.

No matter what a document says." She shivered. And Fargo drew her close. "They're going to kill us, aren't they?"

"They'll try," Fargo said. He pulled her closer, feeling the softness of her. His lips brushed her hair.

"I just want to forget everything," Ernesta said. "I just want to live."

Fargo held her chin and kissed her, drinking in her sweet taste. She wasn't shy, taking his tongue deep into her mouth, opening to him. Her arms moved around him as he held her. She ran her fingers through his hair, and he thought of her face, her dark eyes.

"I thought you were someone special the first time I saw you," she said. "In the chapel, remember?"

She guided his hand to her soft breast. She had laced her dress together where it had been ripped the night before. Now she tugged at the laces until he could slip his hand inside, along her warm silken flesh. Her nipples were hard in his palm, and he felt himself swell and harden.

"Yes," Ernesta breathed in his ear. Her hand moved along his thigh, found him, tight, pressing against the Levi's. "Oh, yes."

Fargo pulled her dress up along her smooth legs, his hand edging along her satiny thigh. She fumbled at his belt buckle and undid his Levi's. He felt her cool hands around his hotness, stroking him lightly, teasingly. His hands moved upward, reached her curly nap and then the wetness within. He explored the warm folds of her as she gasped. Then he slowly inserted his finger into her tight sheath.

"Oh, yes, Skye," she said. "Yes, yes."

Her hips were moving rhythmically against him as if she could not help herself. Suddenly, Ernesta lay back, and he felt her pull her dress off over her head. His hands found her lean body, the narrow hips, the mounds of her breasts, the hard nipples. Fargo knelt between her open legs, hard and ready, and lifted her hips toward him. He slid deeply into her, and then fell forward and felt her warm softness beneath him in the darkness.

She was rising to meet his every movement, as if she could anticipate exactly what he wanted. Her hands twined in his hair and she kissed his ears. Her hips undulated with a slow circular motion that drove him deeper and deeper into her. He could feel her swelling, tighter around him.

"Oh! Oh!"

Her legs came up around his waist as he began to pump into her, feeling the grip of her around him, pressing harder, deeper up into her. Suddenly, she pulled at him and he paused, realizing she wanted to be on top. They rolled over, and she began to ride him, up and down, faster and faster, her sheath contracting around him in exquisite palpitations. Fargo could feel the explosion gathering in him, and then she slowed, moving her hips with excruciating slowness, up and down his long rod. She bent over and kissed him lightly, then took his tongue in her mouth. She began, moving, up down, plunging him in and out of her.

"Ah, ah," she gasped suddenly, and Fargo could feel her contractions begin.

He flipped her over and plunged inside her, driving harder through her steaming slickness, deeper and deeper as the pounding explosion began, like fire and molten gold erupting, pumping into her tightness, then letting go and squirting into her, deeper, again, again, again. At last he slowed and stopped.

Fargo lay beside her and drew her close. She nestled next to him, and he felt the comfort of her soft warmth.

"I'm sorry we had to meet this way," she murmured. "I'm sorry there won't be a second time."

"There will be," Fargo said resolutely, squeezing her as he heard her breathing slip into sleep. He wished he felt more sure when he said that. He lay in the darkness of the box wagon and thought about the Tewa and their land, and Fraco and Lucero. But most of all, he thought abut Gonzalez. Where had the crooked and charismatic priest come from? And why was he so determined to take the Tewa's land and sign it over to Fraco? The whole thing just didn't make sense.

Several hours later Fargo awoke suddenly. The wagon began to move. He got to his feet and dressed quickly.

"What is it? Where are they taking us?" Ernesta asked, struggling into her clothes.

Fargo looked out of the small barred window as the wagon trundled slowly down the streets. Then he saw the central plaza come into view and the front of the chapel. The wagon creaked to a standstill. It was nearly sunset. Ernesta came to stand beside him. She stood on tiptoe to see out. Gonzalez's armed monks were wandering around the plaza. In a few minutes Fargo saw the first of the Tewa arrive for their customary sunset service. In minutes the entire plaza was filled with the tribe. Many of them were so worn down that they simply sat in the dust and stared straight ahead.

"Oh, my people," Ernesta said bitterly. "They are too sick now to even climb to the sacred place on Black Mesa."

The monks seems to be rounding up all the stragglers and driving them to the plaza. Soon the whole tribe of a hundred and fifty Indians was assembled in the plaza. The door of the chapel opened and Padre Gonzalez emerged. He wore a white robe with a gold and silver shawl that fell to his feet with fringe. As usual, his face was not visible beneath the white hood, but a golden crown was on his head. Near him stood two monks holding the bread and wine.

Suddenly, Fargo sighted a familiar stocky figure—Plowright was being led by a monk.

"Hey, Plowright," Fargo shouted to him through the window. The smithy looked all around, and Fargo called out again.

Plowright looked straight at the wagon, and Fargo stuck his hand out of the window and waved. Plowright's face fell as he realized Fargo was locked in the wagon.

"Fargo! What the hell—"

The monk scowled and nudged Plowright along with the barrel of his rifle. They disappeared.

Meanwhile, Gonzalez had begun to distribute the bread and wine. The Indians, sometimes assisted by the monks, staggered forward and received their portion. Then they returned to their places. By the time most of the tribe had received the sacraments, some of them were lying down. One by one, the Tewa families lay down in the dust of the plaza.

"Is he killing my people?" Ernesta asked as they watched. In the darkening dusk more and more of the tribe lay down in the plaza.

"I don't know," Fargo said. Just then, Fargo saw a monk heading their way. There was something familiar about the way he walked. As he came closer, Fargo realized it was Plowright in a monk's robe. The old smithy came up to the door of the wagon and pulled a small saw from his sleeve.

"Have you out in no time," he whispered.

"Do it later," Fargo said in a low voice, trying not to attract the attention of the monks standing nearby.

"Eh?" Plowright said, pausing. The sound of the saw against the metal seemed as loud as thunder. Fargo's view out the window was blocked by Plowright's head as he stood working on the padlock. The situation was impossible, Fargo thought. The old smithy was sure to be noticed and caught red-handed. The sound of the sawing ceased.

"There!" Plowright said, jerking on the padlock.

"Later!" Fargo said. If only the old man would leave them with the padlock sawed away. They couldn't very well just open the door and walk away in front of a plaza full of Gonzalez and his men. Plowright opened the door a little and threw something inside. Fargo felt around for it in the gloom. Monks' robes. It would be a miracle if they could slip out undetected. But hell, it was worth a try.

Fargo and Ernesta slipped into the robes as Plowright stood near the wagon. Fargo took a look out the window. The darkness had fallen, making it hard to see. But the plaza was littered with the dark forms of the Tewa. Maybe no one would notice . . .

He pushed the door open and slipped out, pulling Ernesta behind him. They had taken barely a step when a voice said, "Freeze."

Fargo cursed and wheeled about. Without pausing to think, he jumped the monk standing there, hitting him full force. The rifle discharged, and Fargo went down on top of him, swinging. A hard uppercut to the belly left the man gasping, and a swift left spun his head to one side. Fargo leapt to his feet as the alarm began to spread.

Dark-robed monks came swarming from all directions. One sprang out from behind the other wagon, his rifle spitting fire.

Fargo pushed Ernesta alongside the wagon and dove to the ground. Plowright, caught in the open, spun around. The burst of fire caught him in the belly, and he staggered, then went down. Plowright was dead before he hit the dust.

Fargo cursed and scrambled along the length of the wagon, dragging Ernesta with him, aiming to make a run for it the back way. They dashed across the plaza with gunfire streaming around them, heading for the cover of the dwellings.

"We have to get to the stable," Fargo said, breathing hard. Once on the Ovaro, he knew he could outride any man alive.

They turned a corner and found a stable right ahead. Fargo pursed his lips and whistled. He heard an answering whinny. As they ran toward the stable, he whistled again, but there was no other sound. Fargo and Ernesta dashed inside the dark enclosure that smelled of hay, manure, and horse's sweat. Fargo spotted the Ovaro, and it whinnied furiously. Fargo flung open its stall door. The pinto was hobbled cruelly with iron shackles. Hell, it would take more time to get them off than he had. They'd have to take another horse. He pulled a roan out of a stall, hoping it could fly. No time for a saddle either. Fargo jumped on its back and pulled Ernesta aboard. He spurred the roan and it reared, then cantered out of the stable into the waiting circle of Gonzalez's men. They opened fire, and the air was filled with flying lead. Fargo grabbed Ernesta and rolled off the roan, hitting the hard ground. The scream of the horse filled the air. It faltered and then went down as its terrible voice split the air.

Fargo swore and the rage he had suppressed welled up in him again in a black fury, as if the horse's voice had set something free in him. Lucero dead. Plowright dead. With a roar Fargo raced toward the nearest monk and seized him by the throat, throttling the man. He gurgled, and Fargo felt the windpipe collapse under his iron grip. Rough hands seized him, and he spun about, his powerful right swinging and catching the next monk with a bone-crushing blow to the jaw. The man went down. Rage, red and black, burning flames seemed to consume him. Fargo struck again, a whistling left that caught the next man in his belly and snapped a couple of ribs. A huge man came at him then, Emilio, his eyes like pools of black water.

The others backed off a little, clearing a circle. Emilio crouched warily, then suddenly moved forward, quicker than Fargo would have believed possible for someone his size. Fargo sidestepped, and the big man barreled past. Fargo tripped him and he went down, sprawling in the dust. Fargo threw himself on Emilio, pinning the man to the ground. Even as he did, he knew it was an empty victory. The first blow did not take him by surprise. It came from one of the monks standing around them. A rifle butt across his shoulders, he thought, as the pain exploded across his back and through his bones. Another to the head. Fargo rolled off Emilio and tried to crawl for cover as the blows fell, again and again, as the monks began beating him with their rifles.

"He's mine. I want him alive. Alive."

Through the thickness of pain and the cacophony of the ringing in his ears, Fargo heard the voice again.

"I want him alive."

The voice was Fraco's.

And then all went black.

Fargo opened his eyes and saw the rocky ground swaying beneath him. The up-and-down motion made his head spin. He closed his eyes again.

The next thing he knew, a burning cold splash hit him.

"Wake up," a voice said.

Fargo forced his eyes open. It was night, and cold wind blew against his face, which was wet. The sky was filled with stars and the moon hung like a silver pendant against the black velvet night. Fraco stood in front of him, an empty bucket in his hand.

"That's better," Fraco said.

Fargo winced as he moved his head from side to side. The scene slowly revolved and then came back into focus. He was hurt badly, he knew. His head ached, and he tried to will his hand to his forehead, but it did not seem to obey. It took another moment for Fargo to realize he was upright and shackled, hand and feet. They had brought him up to Black Mesa.

Fargo looked around, trying to keep the scene from spinning. Ernesta was beside him, also in chains. She was staring at him, concern on her face.

"So, I've got you both now," Fraco said, striding up and down in front of them. "Dawn Mountain, the chief's daughter. Too proud, too high and mighty to look at Broken Stick." He grabbed her chin roughly, and she tried to look away from him. "I'll make you pay for that. You'll wish you'd said yes a thousand times. You'll beg me to take you."

"Never!" Ernesta spit at him.

Fraco hit her hard across the face, and although the tears started in her eyes, Fargo saw that she clenched her teeth, refusing to cry out. Hell, she had spirit.

"And you, Mr. Skye Fargo," Fraco said. "Famous

man. Famous for being the good guy. I hate guys like you."

"Mutual," Fargo said.

Fraco cackled. He drew back his arm and then dropped it.

"Why waste my effort?" he said. "I've got all the time in the world. Nobody will come looking for you. And tomorrow morning I'm going to bring all that nice blacksmithing equipment up here. Those bellows, all that metal. And I plan to do me a little branding."

Fraco laughed again and Ernesta gasped.

"You like the sound of that, don't you Dawn Mountain? I'm going to brand my name all over your body. You'll look like one of those white men's cows."

Fargo's head was clear now. He gritted his teeth in fury and tugged at the heavy shackles holding his wrists and ankles. The chains were forged iron, the padlocks thick and strong. There was absolutely no escape this time. And they were at the mercy of a madman.

Fargo heard someone coming up the trail. He was surprised to see the figure of Padre Gonzalez riding on a burro. What the hell had happened down there anyway? The priest dismounted and walked toward them.

"Well, Fraco," Gonzalez said in his deep, oily voice. "You finally have what you wanted. And a bonus, too."

"Oh, yes," Fraco said agreeably. In the presence of Gonzalez Fraco seemed to shrink with fear. "I'll take good care of them. But very slowly. Very slowly."

Gonzalez smiled. He walked over and stood in front of Fargo, looking at him for a long time. The padre's hood was up, and Fargo peered into the deep shadow beneath, but could barely make out the features of the priest's face.

"So, we finally meet, Skye Fargo," Gonzalez said. "For many years I have heard of your reputation. All those years I thought someday I will meet this famous Trailsman. And always, I said to myself, if I ever fail, it will be because of Skye Fargo. But, you see, I was wrong." Gonzalez spread his hands and gestured about at the top of Black Mesa. "I was wrong because I have won and you have lost." He suddenly laughed, a rich throaty laugh. "The end of the trail for Skye Fargo. A fitting finale to my own famous career."

"Career? Just who are you anyway?" Fargo asked.

"Didn't you guess?" Gonzalez said. "Oh, Mr. Fargo. You have disappointed me."

Gonzalez pulled back his hood, and the moonlight streamed across his face. Ernesta screamed. It was a horrible face, misshapen and battered. The skin was pocked and scarred, the nose broken, smashed almost flat. The mouth was a small, cruel cut. The eyes were almost hidden in masses of scar tissue. The man hardly looked human.

"Now do you recognize me?"

Fargo stared at the monstrous face. Something about the eyes reminded him of a picture he'd seen long ago—on a wanted poster.

"Carlos Juarez," Fargo said. "Head of the No-Hand Gang."

"But Juarez died," Ernesta said with a gasp. "He was trapped in the canyon and shot. He fell into the Rio Grande."

"Where he was beaten against the rocks. And he survived," Fargo said, his eyes never leaving Gonzalez. "Barely."

"But . . . but the letters from the Pope in Rome," Ernesta said.

"Forgeries were always a specialty of mine," Juarez said. "And those nuns down in Santa Fe were so stupid, they fell for it, too. And they'll fall again before the night is out."

Fargo didn't like the sound of that. The famous bandido bowed slightly toward them.

"You see, I will have my revenge," Juarez said. "The Tewa tribe helped McMullen track me down. I swore they'd pay. And now they have."

"You've killed them all," Ernesta said. "All my people."

"Oh no, my dear," Juarez said smoothly. "Only put them to sleep. And now all of them are loaded in those wagons you so thoughtfully repaired for us, Mr. Fargo." Juarez pointed down toward the pueblo, and Fargo could see the wagons standing in the empty plaza. "You see, there are gold mines in South America where a slave is worth two hundred gold pieces. And where you can sell a woman for five hundred." Juarez stepped close to Ernesta. "Too bad I can't take you along, too. But in another day or two, after Fraco is done with you, I'm afraid I couldn't give you away." Ernesta shuddered.

"So, you're selling them all into slavery," Fargo said.

"But when the whole tribe turns up missing, somebody will come after you."

"Not likely," Gonzalez said smoothly.

"But people are going to get suspicious, what with Fraco sitting on all this land?"

"Not when I offer to sell it to 'em," the skinny man said. "You see, my tribe all converted and followed their priest down to Mexico to help him found a new mission down there. Wonderful people, my tribe. And they left the land to me to sell piece by piece to the highest bidder. And I send the money down to the mission."

"To Juarez you mean," Fargo said.

"To me, of course," the bandido answered. "And when the last of the land is sold, Fraco will come to join us in our little paradise. No one will ever be able to find me down in South America. And soon, people around here will forget there ever was a tribe called the Tewa. They will have been wiped off the face of the earth." He smiled.

The plan was diabolical. And there was no way to stop it. Juarez, killer of hundreds of innocent men and women and children, would drive the wagons loaded with unconscious Tewa straight down to Mexico. In another two weeks the tribe would all be slaves in some nameless gold mine deep in the jungle, and Juarez would be rich.

"Isn't it wonderful?" Juarez said, as if divining Fargo's thoughts. The bandido pulled up his hood again. "And now it is time for the final act of my performance. My final revenge. Farewell, Ernesta, Fargo. Come, Fraco."

"Until tomorrow," Fraco said, chucking Ernesta under the chin.

Carlos Juarez turned away and mounted his burro. Fraco followed on foot. Fargo watched as they disappeared down the trail.

His head was spinning again, the pain of the beating radiating from all parts of his body. His ribs hurt, and he guessed he'd broken a couple. And there was a sharp stabbing pain in his neck each time he turned his head, as well as a dull throb on his skull where no doubt he had a large goose egg. He flexed his muscles in his arms and legs. Nothing broken. That was a miracle. He was having some trouble seeing out of his left eye though, and he guessed it was swelling shut. Fargo tugged again at the shackles at his hands and feet and examined them again. Solid. He tried to see if he could pull his hand out of the handcuff, but it fit his wrist too tightly. Ernesta was watching him closely.

"Can you pull one of your hands out?" he asked her. "Close your palm tight like this and try."

"I have," she answered in despair. "I can't." Fargo looked closely and could see, even in the moonlight, the blood that dripped down her arms. Yes, she had tried that already. There was nothing to be done. But still Fargo refused to accept defeat. Ernesta wept for a while, quietly as if she were trying to keep him from hearing.

Far below, Fargo heard the sounds of wagons and horses, and he watched as the four wagons pulled out of the pueblo and wound down the trail. They were heading toward Santa Fe and the trail that would take them south to Mexico. Inside the wagons were the hundred and fifty Tewa Indians, bound for the slave mines.

"I don't want to die," she said.

They said no more through the long night. Fargo watched as the moon set. He heard the call of the burrowing owls far down below and the chirp of the pikas among the rocks. Again and again he thought over what Juarez had told him. The bandido had spent several years in hiding, regaining his strength and plotting the way to make a fortune and to wreak his revenge on the Tewa. Ernesta slept off and on, fitfully.

Dawn brightened apricot and gold. Fargo watched it with appreciation, wondering how many more times he'd see the sun rise. He stopped the thought. Ernesta awoke and groaned.

"My arms," she said. "I'm hurting so much. I can't feel my hands any more."

Fargo tried once again with the shackles, jerking at each one with his hand or foot. But each of them held.

The sun mounted higher, and they heard someone coming up the slope.

"I'm afraid," Ernesta said.

"Forget your fear," Fargo said. "If the worst happens, just remember how much you hate him. That will help you bear the pain."

Fargo looked over and saw her bite her lip. A look of resolve came into her eyes. If they were going to die on this butte, he was sure she would fight until the very end. Fraco appeared on a burro loaded with saddlebags.

"Good morning," he said. He dismounted and stretched in the sun, then took the cap off his canteen.

"Would you like some water?" he asked Ernesta. He approached, holding the canteen out toward her lips. Then he snatched it back. "No, I think I'll wait a few days. And then maybe I'll give you a drop. They say your tongue turns black and hangs out of your mouth."

"Don't listen," Fargo said.

"What else do you have to do?" Fraco asked with an evil smile.

He unloaded the burro, and Fargo saw what he had feared. The madman was making good on his promise of the day before. He began by making a firepit and piling it with wood. Then he removed tongs and other implements from the saddlebags. Fargo watched the man, studying his every movement. If he could only find a weak spot. Find a way to . . . to what? Nevertheless, it was his only hope. Back and forth, Fraco went, laying the fire and spreading out the implements. Finally, he pulled out a tinderbox.

The wind was blustery on top of the mesa, and for a minute Fargo's hopes rose in him. The fire wasn't going to light. But after a few tries, Fraco got the kindling burning, and soon an orange flame danced in the wind. He positioned the tongs in the fire, intending to use them as a brand. Fraco paced up and down and in front of them again, then stood before Ernesta.

"Ladies first," he said. He ran a finger down the inside of her forearm. "We'll start here. And then we'll go on to other, more interesting places."

"Why don't you start with me?" Fargo said. "You worm."

Fraco stopped in his tracks and turned about slowly.

"I have somewhere very special in mind for you," he said. "But I'll start with her."

"Why? Haven't got the guts?"

Fargo knew he was playing a dangerous game—taunting a man who held the means of torture. Still, it was their only chance. Maybe Fraco would get angry. Would make a mistake.

"I've heard enough from you," Fraco said. He fetched two gags from the saddlebags and tied them on. Then he knelt by the fire, turning the metal tongs.

"Why aren't they red yet?" he muttered. Fargo knew the tongs were made of a special alloy that would not melt at high temperatures. But the tongs were plenty hot. Hot enough to burn badly. But Fraco didn't know that. "Bellows," he said. "I need bellows." He went to the saddlebags and riffled through them impatiently. Then he cursed and peered over in the direction of the pueblo far below. He seemed to hesitate a moment, then made up his mind.

"I'll be back soon," he announced. "I want to do this right."

Fraco mounted the burro and set off down the trail again. An hour, Fargo thought. They had gained an hour at most.

As soon as Fraco disappeared, Ernesta began to pull at her shackles desperately. Above her gag her eyes were wild with fear. Her wrists and ankles began bleeding again as the sharp metal bit into her flesh.

Fargo watched the fire. It burned lower and lower to embers. The coals fell and turned white. The flames died down and then snuffed out in the wind. A puff of white smoke rose. Time had passed and he had thought of no solution. Ernesta had given up her struggle and she was sobbing quietly. Fargo heard the sound of Fraco returning—the hoofs on the trail, then the creak of leather as he dismounted. Footsteps nearer and nearer, then stopping.

Fargo looked up, surprised to see the tall stranger in black standing in front of him. Black eyes glittered above a broken nose. The man drew his silver pistol and aimed it straight at Fargo.

"Well, I finally caught up with you," he said. "You're a helluva hard man to catch, but I've done it."

Fargo tried to speak, but the gag muffled his words. If only he could bargain with the man, whoever he was. Try to get him to see reason.

"Don't give me any excuses," the stranger said. "I've had about as much trouble finding you as I'm going to stand."

Ernesta screamed as the man raised the barrel of his gun and pulled the trigger. As the gunshot exploded, Fargo's last thought was that at least he'd die fast.

6

The shot resounded against the rocks. Ernesta screamed again.

Fargo felt the jolt against his wrist—the jolt of the release of his arm as the chain was shot off. The stranger raised his gun and fired again, a sure shot and both Fargo's arms were free. Fargo untied his gag. The tall stranger didn't pause, but fired at the chains holding Ernesta's ankles, freeing her as well.

"I sure did have a hard time keeping up with you," the stranger said, turning back to him. "Been tracking you through Montana, down in Cheyenne, and out to Kansas. Then you slipped on down this way, but I missed you again in Taos. Some kid told me you'd headed north to Ute country, but I knew he was lying. Figured you'd be heading on south to Santa Fe. But say, you look like you been through hell and back. You got yourself in a bad pickle." He glanced toward the poles where the chains dangled and then at the firepit, still smoking a little. "I rode into this pueblo yesterday, and some monk showed me your horse, but he was being pretty close-mouthed about where you were. I figured something bad was up, so I thought I'd do some looking around. They were acting funny so I figured they had you prisoner or something."

"Who are you?" Fargo rasped. His throat was dry.

"Oh, sorry," the stranger said. He offered his hand. "My name's McMullen. Folks call me Mac."

"You're the marshal that rode down Carlos Juarez up on the Rio Grande," Fargo said.

"Yeah, that's me," Mac said, looking abashed. "He killed my brother up in Durango, and I swore I'd get him. Did, too. In fact it's because of Juarez I've been looking for you, Fargo. Now, you may find this hard to believe but—"

"He's alive," Fargo cut in. "Juarez is alive."

"You heard that rumor, too?" Mac asked, scratching his head.

"It's more than a rumor," Fargo said. "It's true. Carlos Juarez was standing right where you are just last night. But by now he may be halfway to Mexico."

"Damn!" Mac swore, stamping the ground. "Well hell, Fargo. I came looking for you because I thought you could help me track him down if anybody could. But looks like you already done it. Excuse me, I'm forgetting. You want some water or something, lady?"

Ernesta was sitting on a rock, looking dazed. Mac handed her his canteen, and she took it gratefully.

"You must have run into a skinny guy down below," Fargo said.

"Didn't see anybody," Mac said. "Whole Indian pueblo down there is completely deserted."

"How'd you find us?"

Mac pointed to the wisp of smoke rising from the smoldering fire.

Fargo wondered where Fraco had got to. Maybe he'd seen Mac riding in and had been surprised without a weapon. Maybe he'd taken cover. Or maybe he was now heading back up the Black Mesa trail. But he surely would have heard the gunfire and he'd be on his guard.

"One of Juarez's scum is still hanging around here," Fargo said. Ernesta shivered and passed him the canteen and he took a swig, and then another. "He's the one who put us in these chains. You got an extra gun?"

"Sure," Mac said. Fargo took the long-barreled Colt Army that Mac handed him. They walked over to look down the trail and see if anything was moving in the pueblo below.

"Well, look at that. There he goes," Mac said as they saw a small figure run across the plaza and enter the chapel. "Think he's going to pray?"

"They had a load of rifles in there," Fargo said. "Unless they took them all to Mexico. Maybe he heard the gunshots and went to get one."

"Let's go hunt a rat," Mac said.

While Mac stood watching for any more movement down below, Fargo cut the shackles off their wrists and ankles, using the tools Fraco had left by the fire. They put Ernesta on Mac's horse and started the descent. Fargo kept his eyes on the church, but Fraco never reappeared. As far as he knew there was only the one door in front so he was probably still inside. As they hurried down the trail, Fargo felt the deep bruises and stiffness in his muscles and joints. He'd been beaten badly, but the worst of it had been hanging by his arms all night. His shoulders were tight. The movement of the brisk walk downhill was working the kinks out though.

They reached the plaza. Fargo considered leaving Ernesta somewhere, but realized that if Fraco had escaped from the church, he might take her hostage, and he decided they should stick together. Mac gave Ernesta his silver derringer just in case, and the three of them slid along the front of the church.

Fargo burst through the door first, Colt in hand. The chapel was empty. With the Colt high before him and his finger tight on the trigger, he called the others in after him. Ernesta and Mac took cover behind the columns as Fargo dashed down the aisle and kicked the small door beside the altar that led to the inner sanctum. It didn't budge. He stepped back and shot at the lock once, twice, then kicked at it. The door sprang open. Fargo poked his head around the corner and withdrew it quickly. The gun rack was empty. One of the tables had been upended though and lay on its side. Fargo was willing to bet good money that Fraco was cowering on the other side.

"Come out with your hands up, Fraco," Fargo shouted. There was a long silence, and Fargo considered their next move. He heard a rustle inside. Mac dashed up the aisle and slid along the wall on the other side of the door.

"He's in there all right," Mac said in a conversational tone of voice. "I saw him looking up over that table. I'm guessing he doesn't have any bullets, though. Or else he'd have shot at us already." Mac removed his hat and winked at Fargo. "Let's rush him on the count of three."

"One, two—" said Fargo.

Mac threw his hat across the doorway. Four shots rang out and the hat fell to the ground.

"Good try, Fraco," Fargo said.

Fargo popped around the corner and pumped six bullets into the room, just to shake him up. Mac tossed Fargo more ammo and he reloaded the Colt.

"How long you think he'll hold out?" Mac said. "We've got a lot of bullets."

"Come on, Fraco. If you come out with your hands in the air," Fargo said, "you'll get a jury trial down in Santa Fe." There was the sound of a rustle again. "Throw your gun where we can see it," Fargo instructed. They heard the sound of the gun sliding across the floor, and a silver Vaquero appeared in the doorway. Mac looked surprised. "Good. Now stand up real slowly, hands in the air." Fargo looked around the corner and saw Fraco rise from behind the overturned table.

Fargo stepped into the room and as he did, the skinny man suddenly contracted downward like a snake about to strike and reached inside his shirt. Fargo fired, catching Fraco in the belly just as his hand came out with a derringer. Fraco fell, face first onto the stone. When he hit the floor, his own gun discharged again, straight into his chest. It was over.

Ernesta came up to stand behind Fargo, and she looked at Fraco's body for a long time as if to convince herself that he was really dead.

"Let's go," Fargo said. "We've got to get to Santa Fe and get some help. Then we've got to run down Juarez."

Fargo retrieved his Henry rifle from the roof of the adobe dwelling where he'd hidden it and filled the chambers and his pockets full of extra bullets from McMullen. They found two palominos in the stable for Fargo and Ernesta.

They rode hard on the trail to Santa Fe. On the way Fargo told Mac all about the happenings at Black Mesa.

"Just how many men does he have?" Mac asked.

Fargo thought hard, counting up all the different monks he'd noticed at the pueblo.

"I'd estimate about a dozen." Ernesta confirmed his count. Mac looked thoughtful.

"You know, we hung that No-Hand Gang in Santa Fe," Mac said. "Now, it's a helluva world when a bandido can get another gang of no-goods together so quick."

Fargo agreed, his thoughts on the wagon train heading south. Every hour that passed meant Carlos Juarez and his gang were closer to the Mexican border. And once he slipped into that country, it would be almost impossible to find him. As the afternoon light was turning to gold, they reached Santa Fe.

Mac and Ernesta headed to the cantina to try to round up some men for a posse. Fargo went to the Governor's Palace and burst into the office. The bespectacled clerk stared up at him.

"The sheriff—where is he?" Fargo asked.

"Gone. He and the whole posse went north to Taos

to help chase down some cattle rustlers. Bunch of thieves up there. They won't be back until day after tomorrow."

"Where can I find some men?" Fargo snapped.

"I dunno," he said with a shrug. Fargo banged out the door and heard the clerk calling after him. "But . . . but you've got no legal authority to round up a posse. Hey! Hey you!"

Fargo strode across the plaza toward the cantina. Mac stood arguing with a bunch of men who were sitting around a barrel on the porch, drinking beer. The men were trail-worn, wagon train drovers by the looks of them.

"I tell you, Carlos Juarez is alive and heading to Mexico," Mac said hotly.

"Oh, go on," one of the men said with a dismissive gesture. "Carlos Juarez died years ago. I read all about it."

Mac groaned, exasperated. "I tell you, he's alive."

"Long as he's not heading this way," another said and belched.

"Well, if he's headed down to Mexico," a third put in, "just let the Mexicans take care of him."

"Goddamn lily-livers," Mac said. Ernesta twisted her hands in dismay. There was nothing they could say to persuade the men to join in the hunt for Juarez.

Fargo spotted a dark-frocked figure slumped over a table in the back. He went over and picked up the man's head. It was Padre Amado Fernandez. And he was drunk.

"Hey, Father," Fargo slapped his face. "What are

you doing here?" He pulled the old priest to his feet. Fernandez opened his blurry eyes and then recognized Fargo.

"Oh, Fargo," he said, his voice slurred. "Well, I've lost everything now. Everything."

"Yeah," Fargo said impatiently.

"Even Desideria," Fernandez said. "My darling, darling girl. He's taken her, too. Gone. Took all my Tewa. And my girl."

Fargo suddenly remembered with a feeling of dread what Carlos Juarez had said about the nuns—that they would soon suffer his revenge as well. "What are you talking about?" Fargo said, shaking the priest. "Who took Desideria?"

Fernandez hiccuped.

"Why, his Holy of Holies, Padre Claudio Gon . . . Gonzalez." Padre Fernandez nearly fell over as Fargo let go of him. What the hell was going on? Juarez and his gang had made off with Desideria as well?

Fargo hurried the padre out of the cantina and called to Mac and Ernesta to follow. Fargo hurried them toward the convent, just a block away.

"There wasn't one goddamn man in that cantina willing to help," Mac muttered bitterly.

When they reached the convent, Fargo shouted and beat on the front gate. There was no answer. He shouted again and finally heard a door open and footsteps crossing the garden court. The gate opened an inch and Fargo saw the pinched face of Sister Alva.

"Where's Desideria?" Fargo asked.

Sister Alva looked surprised and glanced from one

to the other of them. At the sight of Padre Fernandez with his red nose, she shook her head disapprovingly.

"Why they've been called to help out in the new mission in Mexico. Just for a month. To help teach the children. The Holy Father wrote himself that he thought it would be a good experience for the young ladies. And Padre Gonzalez—"

"Young ladies?" Fargo said. "You mean all of them?"

"Why yes," Sister Alva said. "Everyone except the Mother Superior and myself. I volunteered to go, of course, but the dear padre said he would save me for another, more important mission."

"Goddamn," Fargo said. Sister Alva gasped, and Fargo pushed past her into the courtyard. "Where's the Mother Superior?"

Sister Alva was shocked beyond protest. She closed the gate behind them and pointed toward the door. Fargo crossed the courtyard swiftly and found the Mother Superior praying in her room.

"Mr. Fargo," she said, rising, "what brings you here?"

"I hear Gonzalez has made off with all the girls," Fargo said.

"If you mean Padre Gonzalez," the Mother Superior said, "and if you mean he has been ordered by the Pope to take them to a mission—"

"Enough," Fargo said. "He's not a padre. He's Carlos Juarez, head of the No-Hand Gang. And he didn't die up on the Rio Grande. He floated down the river, and he's been forging documents and posing as a padre in order to take the Tewa land and sell all the

Indians as slaves down in Mexico. And he'll sell the girls into slavery, too. Or worse."

The Mother Superior went white as she tried to take in the news. Her knees buckled under her, and she started to sink. Sister Alva rushed forward and slid a chair under her. The Mother Superior gaped like a fish out of water for a minute or two.

"Carlos Juarez," Sister Alva said triumphantly. "Padre Gonzalez is really Carlos Juarez? I always knew there was something amiss about Gonzalez." Sure, Fargo thought. He didn't bother to remind the old woman about her complete adoration of the padre.

"My God," Padre Fernandez said, crossing himself. "Oh, my God." Fargo looked at the old man who was flushing red as a beet. "Carlos Juarez has kidnapped his own daughter," the padre said. "Desideria is his daughter, you see. A young woman in my parish in California . . . he was young and she . . . she died in childbirth. Juarez never knew about the child, but I brought her up as my own."

The Mother Superior gaped again, unable to speak.

"I knew it!" Sister Alva said. "Desideria is daughter of a bandit. I knew there was always something lawless about that girl."

"Shut up," Fargo snapped.

"And I let him take the girls," Mother Superior said. "I let Carlos Juarez kidnap those innocent girls. I saw the document and I believed him."

"No, it's my fault," Padre Fernandez said. "I was

not a good guardian to the girl. This is God's punishment."

"Shut up both of you," Fargo said. "Mac and I are going after them. As soon as we find some more guns."

"Doesn't seem to be anybody in Santa Fe willing," Mac said.

The Mother Superior raised her head, and a light came into her keen blue eyes. "What do you mean?" she said, rising to her feet. "I'm willing."

"I don't think so, ma'am," Mac said, looking at her skeptically. "I've chased this bastard . . . beg your pardon . . . down before."

"I can ride and I can shoot," the Mother Superior said. "I was raised on a ranch. I'm coming with you."

"Well, so am I," said Padre Fernandez.

"I guess I'll come, too," Sister Alva said.

"This is ridiculous," Fargo said, looking around at them. "Mac and I are going to ride after Carlos Juarez with two nuns and a priest."

"And me, too," Ernesta said. "I'm coming. Those are my people in those wagons, and I'll do anything to save them."

Fargo looked helplessly at Mac.

"We ain't going to find a posse in Santa Fe," Mac said. "And the way I figure it, we need every gun we can get, no matter who's holding it. Every minute we stay here, that bandido's closer to Mexico."

"Well, then, let's go get the bastard!" Sister Alva said.

"Sister!" admonished Mother Superior.

"Oh, hell," Fargo said. "Come on. Let's get saddled up."

The Mother Superior and Sister Alva took the convent's horses. They were surprisingly good mounts, Fargo saw with relief. They also found a horse for Padre Fernandez who left his burro behind in the stable. Fargo had his Henry rifle, and Mac carried a similar model. Mac handed his Army Colt to Ernesta and two extra hunting rifles to the padre and the Mother Superior. Sister Alva got a small derringer.

As Fargo rode out, leading the six of them south on the road to Mexico, he turned about and watched them following. The nuns and the padre rode surprisingly well, he saw, as did Ernesta. Still, it was a damned strange posse to run down the likes of Carlos Juarez. But there was no choice. And there was no time to do any better.

Fargo turned about and concentrated his mind on the battle ahead of them. Twelve armed and desperate men loyal to Carlos Juarez. Four wagons full of innocent Tewa and girls from the convent. The miles sped by as he thought of strategy. Where was the weak point they could turn to their advantage?

The land descended from the high Santa Fe plateau to the drier desert land to the south. This was the trickiest part of the trail, the long descent to the flat desert below, a steep grade that was hard enough to get up and even harder to get down. The horses picked their way down the slope.

He thought of the trail ahead. After the steep descent, Carlos Juarez would probably take the old Spanish trail, the Camino Real, that led straight south along the Rio Grande. A wagon could travel fast along the trail—but not as fast as six riders, Fargo thought.

He patted the neck of the palomino. It was a sturdy horse, but nothing compared to his black-and-white pinto, the powerful Ovaro. Fargo wondered what was happening to his horse and how Juarez was treating it.

He turned around and saw he'd pulled ahead of the group. He slowed the palomino down until they caught up. Mac, on his powerful chestnut, brought up the rear just in case of trouble. The sun set and the stars came out. They galloped on through the long evening, only pausing occasionally to water the horses and let them cool down. Then they were on the trail again.

As the moon rose, Fargo saw the thin grasslands around them and the distant mountains receding in the distance. It was nearly dawn when they paused in the little town of Albuquerque. Fargo pulled up in front of an adobe dwelling where a sign promised GOOD GRUB. He dismounted and pounded on the door. After a few minutes an oil lamp was lit inside and a grouchy voice called out. Fargo pounded on the door again.

The door opened an inch, and Fargo saw a man in his nightshirt with a rifle.

"You got some trouble, stranger?" the man asked.

"Yeah," Fargo said. "We're trying to find some monks. It's an emergency. The sisters, here," Fargo said, jerking his thumb over his shoulder toward where the Mother Superior and Sister Alva sat on their horses. He decided it was just too confusing to explain about Carlos Juarez. Nobody would believe them anyway.

"Oh, yeah," said the man scratching his head. "Well, they're right ahead of you. I bet you catch 'em up by midday. Came through here an hour after midnight. Left a bunch of wagons out on the road. Seemed to be in a big hurry. Guess they had a hard time on old Heartbreak Hill."

"Thanks," Fargo said. He related the news to the others. The wagons had had a hard time descending the steep grade from the plateau. And Juarez had lost valuable time. Now Fargo realized they would have to change their strategy. He would have to ride out a mile ahead to find Juarez and the wagon train, leaving Mac in charge of the group. That way, he could scope out the situation and plan the attack.

Fargo mounted again, and they sped off down the trail. They didn't have much of a chance, he realized. The coming battle would be bloody and hard. And they were outnumbered and outgunned. The only thing they had going for them was that Juarez was not expecting an attack. As far as Carlos Juarez knew, Fargo was chained to the top of Black Mesa at the mercy of Fraco.

He rode on through the long morning, eyes and ears alert. The land grew drier, the sage giving way to prickly pear and sparse yellow grass. The red dusty mountains in the distance turned to angular buttes, cut by the wind and rain. As the white sun climbed, the sky grew pale with the blasting heat. They were still a couple day's fast ride to the Mexican border.

Fargo had just paused at the top of a rise when he

saw the dust plume ahead. There they were. His keen eyes picked out the shapes of the four lumbering wagons and the dark forms of the horsed men who rode in a swarm around the wagon train. Fargo felt the rage rise in him, but he turned it ice cold as he sat remembering what the land was like farther south.

Yes, there was a place he remembered from years before—a place he'd camped out one night on the trail. The hills pinched inward toward the river, and red rocks rose like towers on all sides. The perfect spot for an ambush. Anyone on the trail below was completely exposed. It was a few hours ahead. Fargo wondered if he could get there in time.

A few minutes later, Mac rode up, leading the rest of the group. They all looked tired, except for Mac. But when Fargo pointed to the smudge on the horizon ahead, Ernesta's eyes grew bright, and the two nuns flushed with excitement. The padre, sober now, drew his revolver and looked at it thoughtfully. Then Fargo led them off the trail into the hills. For the next few hours they bushwhacked through the back country, staying off the trail. It was hard going through the brush. The horses balked at times, but they drove them onward, up and over the hills above the river.

Finally, in midafternoon, Fargo spotted the red rock formations in the hills around them and calculated that they had reached the spot. He turned back toward the Rio Grande, and they rode until he spotted the glint of water shining through a gap in the hills before them. Fargo gave the signal, and they all dismounted and moved forward toward the red rocks that overlooked the trail below.

Fargo saw that he'd overshot the spot he'd been thinking of. It lay a good quarter mile to the north where the river narrowed between the overhanging hills. He was just about to give the signal to them to move northward into position over the gap when he saw a flicker of movement along the trail.

"Hell," Fargo said. A lone rider—in a monk's robe—was coming through the gap to the north. Even from this distance Fargo could see that the man was wary, looking upward toward the red rocks, his rifle held ready. It was clear that they were anticipating an ambush. He was followed by a second rider, just as wary.

"Looks like they're ready to get jumped," Mac said. "And that's a damn good place to jump somebody. Wish we were up there."

There was no time to get into better position, Fargo realized. He instructed everyone to get cover behind the rocks as he watched what happened at the gap. A third rider appeared followed by the first wagon, bristling with men and rifles. In the lead position, pulling the wagon, was the Ovaro.

Fargo felt his hopes sink. Juarez and his men were riding armed and in full readiness for attack. The second wagon came through the gap, followed closely by the third and fourth. Fargo could only imagine what it was like for the Tewa and the convent girls, jammed inside those hot, airless wagons.

Then suddenly, the man riding out in front stopped and turned back, shouting something to the others. It was too far to hear what he said, but Fargo saw the men jump down off the wagons. Some of them left their rifles behind. Several of the riders dismounted and others returned their rifles to their saddle scabbards.

"By God," Mac said. "They were ready to get attacked at the gap. But they didn't, and now they think they're safe. Hell, Fargo." Mac slapped him on the back. "Why you're a right wily fellow. I'd never 'uv thought of hitting 'em right where they'd relax their guard."

"Just lucky," Fargo said.

He passed the word along to the rest of them to shoot at his signal. Twelve "monks"—if he and Mac could take out three each on the first round, that would even the odds some. He watched as the wagons rumbled along, the gang relaxed now, certain they had passed by the most dangerous part of the trail. They walked along, talking with each other. Fargo searched for Juarez and finally spotted him. The bandido rode, still dressed in his priest's robe, but with his head bared. Fargo's finger inadvertently tightened on the trigger of his Henry as he watched the bandido ride along beside the muddy red waters of the Rio Grande. He positioned the barrel of the rifle on the rock in front of him and aimed at the figure of Juarez down below. The first shot would be for him. Fargo glanced over at Mac and saw that he was aiming for Juarez, too. Well, what the hell.

The wagons came closer and closer, and they could hear the creaking of the joints. Any moment now, Fargo thought. He looked around at the others. The

Mother Superior knelt behind a rock, holding the hunting rifle in front of her, squinting down the barrel. She looked like she knew what she was doing with a gun, Fargo thought with surprise. Padre Fernandez crouched nearby. He glanced at Fargo and smiled. Ernesta sat with the Colt resting on her lap, her eyes on the wagons below. Sister Alva perched on a rock, holding the derringer and a couple of bullets in her hands. She appeared to be trying to figure out how to load it. She clicked open the derringer, snapped it shut and, as she did so, squeezed the trigger. The shot echoed through the rocks, followed by Sister Alva's surprised shriek.

Mac fired immediately, and Fargo stared down the barrel of his rifle toward Juarez, who slumped sideways on his horse. Fargo squeezed off a shot and saw the famous bandido jump with the impact of the bullet, then slide off his horse. Fargo shifted his aim immediately to one of the men nearby and plugged him in the belly before the man could draw the rifle out of his saddle scabbard. As the gunfire erupted all around him, he aimed at a third man running for cover and fired. The man's head exploded in a shower of red and his body pitched sideways, sprawled across some rocks.

There was mass confusion below. Juarez's men were scattering in all directions, running for the rocks. The horses were stampeding away in a panic. Fargo heard screams from inside the wagons, and he hoped to hell none of the flying bullets would penetrate the heavy wooden sides. The bullets began whining around them as the gang realized where they were hiding and began returning their fire. A shot whizzed by Fargo's ear and ricocheted through the rocks.

"I think we got about four left down there," Mac shouted above the noise. Fargo aimed and fired, catching another man who was dashing from one rock to another.

"Make that three," he said. But all the men were under cover now. And he couldn't see just where. The river banks had plenty of rocks and a stand of cottonwoods off to one side. They'd have to find them and pick them off one by one now.

The Mother Superior was firing and reloading like some kind of machine gone mad even though she hadn't hit anything yet. Sister Alva had fainted. Ernesta took aim and fired, winging a man who was cowering under the wagon. Padre Fernandez was reloading his rifle.

"Hold your fire," Fargo called out.

"Look! Look!" Ernesta screamed, pointing downward.

Mac cursed, and Fargo glanced down to see the bloodied form of a man on the muddy bank crawling toward the red waters of the Rio Grande. Mac pulled up his rifle and fired once, twice, again. Just as the form slipped into the waters.

"Goddamn it!" Mac swore. "He's done it again. He's not going to get away this time. I'm going down there."

"Not alone," Fargo said. "Hold your fire up here," he told the others. All he and Mac needed was to get killed by their own side.

They dashed from rock to rock, descending the slope. Below, all remained quiet. Too quiet. Fargo wondered if the three remaining men had managed to stay together. They came to the bottom of the slope and still the hidden bandidos had not fired. Good strategy, Fargo thought. Because once they fired, he'd know right where they were.

Fargo's eyes swept the scene, the bodies littering the red mud. And where the hell was Juarez? The famous bandido had slipped into the river like a crocodile, and he was floating downstream out of their reach. The fury rose in him as he and Mac crouched behind the last of the rocks before the open space where the wagons were.

"Where the hell are they?" Mac asked.

A blast of bullets answered his question. The lead poured in around them, whining off the rocks, thudding into the muddy earth. The three men were holed up in a clump of rocks on the far side of the clearing.

"If we just had some cover to get across this space," Mac said, gazing toward the river. It would be suicide to go after Juarez until they cleaned out the last three bandidos. Crossing the open space, they'd be sitting ducks. Fargo looked around desperately. The wagons stood to one side of the clearing, the horses pulling against the traces, confused and frightened by the gunfire. Only the black-and-white pinto stood still.

Fargo whistled. The horse's ears came around, hearing the noise above the clatter of the gunfire. He whistled again and the horse started forward. The two horses behind didn't want to follow, but the Ovaro turned its head and neighed, pulling again. The team started forward hesitantly, the wagon creaking and swaying as the pinto brought it around in a wide circle of the clearing. Fargo could hear the cries of the people inside. The gunfire from the bandidos sputtered to a halt as they watched, not knowing what was going on.

"Neat trick," Mac said appreciatively. Just as the wagon passed by, Fargo and Mac jumped onto the side of it, clinging to iron rings and chains that secured the water barrels hanging underneath. The wagon continued in its circle, heading back to where the bandidos were hiding. As the far side came around to their view, the bandidos opened up their fire, but there was nobody there. The firing stopped as the wagon continued on and just then, Fargo and Mac appeared on the top of the wagon, firing down on the three men crouched in the circle of protecting rock.

Fargo hit the first one in the neck, and the man's blood spouted like a fountain. The second one fired, and the bullet split the air between Fargo and Mac before Mac plugged him in the chest. He fell backward, hitting the third man whose pistol barrel was knocked sideways, the bullet flying wide. Fargo shot him in the head. Just then he spotted the gun in the man's hand. He leapt down and picked it up. It was his own Colt.

"Let's go!" Fargo shouted. He and Mac sprinted across the clearing toward the river. At the bank they saw the bloody track leading down into the wide red river where Juarez had dragged himself into the water. The river was low this time of year. Mac narrowed his eyes and a hard look came into his face.

"I'll ford to the other side of the river," he said. "We'll each take one bank. And we'll keep going until we find the bastard."

"Suits me," Fargo said. Mac forded and then swam across the red river, holding onto a floating log and holding his rifle out of the water. Fargo heard voices calling from the hill above and cries from inside the wagons. "You can come on down now," he called to them. Then he headed down the bank of the river.

It was hard going. Fargo waded in the shallows for a while, his keen eyes sweeping the bank for any trace that Juarez had crawled out of the river. He watched every floating log as it went by, trying to see if was floating free or if Juarez might be hanging on. A tangle of sticks and leaves floated by, and Fargo waded out to intercept it, but Juarez was not floating underneath. From time to time, he glanced up to see Mac searching the shallows and the far bank.

They had gone half a mile when Fargo came on a stretch where the red rocks came right down to the water. The perfect place to get out without leaving tracks. But there were tracks. Fargo saw a few subtle dark spots where moisture—river water or blood—was rapidly drying in the hot sun. Another couple of minutes and the rock would have been dry. Silently, Fargo signaled to Mac, pointing to the rock. The marshall raced upstream, and then swam across again with a log, the current carrying him to where Fargo stood. He emerged dripping wet, holding his dry rifle, his black eyes bent on revenge.

Fargo wordlessly pointed to the dim spots of moisture on the red rock, and Mac's eyes traveled up the red rock toward a tangle of willows, an impenetrable thicket. Together, they silently walked toward it. Through silent looks, Mac told Fargo he was going in first. The willows were bent and crushed where Juarez had crawled into them and fresh blood glistened on some of the leaves. Fargo stood to one side as Mac pushed aside the leaves with the barrel of his rifle.

Suddenly, Mac's rifle was jerked forward. He fired and Fargo fired blind into the thicket. Mac pulled his rifle backward, then fired again and again into the dense leaves. He moved the leaves aside again and Fargo saw the boots of Juarez. Mac fired again, then dragged the body out of the thicket.

This time Carlos Juarez was really dead, his chest a bloody mass, his eyes a staring blankness in his scarred, inhuman face. Mac positioned his rifle over the chest of Juarez and fired one more time. The corpse jumped.

"I think he's dead now," Mac said. "Let's get back. I'm going to take his body back to Santa Fe and get him hung in the main square. Then I'm going to get a picture of it." That reminded Fargo of something. He fished in his pocket and pulled out the slender silver case he'd taken off McMullen the night he jumped him in the alley. As he handed it over, McMullen's face registered surprise.

"That was you?" Mac said. "Hell, Fargo. You're slipprier than I thought."

They walked back to the clearing in silence. When they arrived, they found that Ernesta had managed to unlock the wagons and free all the Tewa and the convent girls. All of the prisoners had run down to the river to drink and to bathe, to cool off from the heat inside the prison wagons.

The Mother Superior and Sister Alva stood watching the young women splashing and laughing in the shallow water. The girls had hiked their dresses up and some had removed their shirts, leaving only their camisoles.

"They really shouldn't be exposing themselves that way," said Sister Alva. "Why, it's indecent."

"Shut up," the Mother Superior said pleasantly. She walked down the bank, kicked off her shoes, and hiked up her habit, wading into the water with the rest of the girls.

"Well!" Sister Alva said.

Fargo stood watching everyone playing and laughing in the cool water of the river. He felt a soft hand on his arm.

"Thank you, Skye."

He turned to see Ernesta looking up at him gratefully.

"The Tewa are safe. Now that Fraco is gone. Now that Padre Gonzalez, I mean Carlos Juarez, is dead. And the land will belong to us forever."

Fargo smiled down at her and took her in his arms. He kissed her warm mouth.

"You see, there *will* be a second time," he said.

Ernesta smiled up at him.

"Skye! Skye!" He looked up to see Desideria standing before him, one hand on her hip and her dark eyes flashing to see him holding another woman. Ernesta laughed, embarrassed, and stepped away from him. Desideria smiled and grabbed his arm.

"Come down to the river," she said, tugging at him. Fargo shot a helpless look over his shoulder toward Ernesta. "I want you to meet the girls. Everybody!" Desideria called out. "This is the man I was telling you about. This is Skye Fargo."

A shriek went up from the river, and all the young women started toward him, giggling. The Mother Superior shouted at them to behave themselves.

Fargo had a feeling his troubles were just beginning.

LOOKING FORWARD!
The following is the opening
section from the next novel in the exciting
Trailsman series from Signet:

**THE TRAILSMAN #168
KIOWA COMMAND**

*1860, where the southwest territory,
a harsh, untamed and vengeful land,
is witness to a devil's bargain
of savagery and death . . . .*

They were near. Not more than two ridges away, he estimated. The big man with the lake blue eyes let a silent oath escape the tight line of his lips. He hadn't liked the job from its outset. Getting closer to the end of it didn't help any. He carried two reasons for disliking the assignment. He never enjoyed working for the army. They were always so damn heavy-handed. Instead of listening to those who knew better, they invariably bulled their way, too often losing their quarry and always unnecessarily losing lives. They probably couldn't help it, Skye Fargo told himself. The military mind was set in its ways, immovable and unimaginative, governed by rules and regulations, bogged down by outmoded

Excerpt from KIOWA COMMAND

tactical manuals designed for another time and another place.

Even a general as smart and flexible as Miles Stanford was not entirely able to free himself from indoctrinated rigidness, Fargo reflected unhappily. So much for the first reasons for his general sourness. The second one was that he disliked trailing renegades, especially renegade Indians. They were as unpredictable as the army was predictable. In dealing with the Indian it was vital to know the differences in tribal codes and tribal behavior. Those were things that could spell the difference in keeping your scalp and losing it. But renegades were outcasts. They had turned their back on their own people. They lived by their own formless rules that were beyond knowing. Yet he was here, Fargo swore silently, thanks to General Miles Stanford. Damn the man, Fargo muttered. He was an old friend who always found a way to prevail on him.

Fargo pushed aside further complaining to scan the ground in front of him. He had been trailing the band of renegades for more than three weeks since he'd left General Stanford's headquarters on the border of the Colorado–New Mexico territory and now he felt a grim satisfaction gather inside himself. They were indeed not far ahead, Fargo murmured as he swung from the magnificent Ovaro to step carefully along the oblong stretch of ground beside a stand of blackjack oak. Skye Fargo studied the ground with the practiced and special eyes of the trailsman, see-

Excerpt from KIOWA COMMAND

ing where others only looked, understanding what others failed to comprehend. The renegades had camped here, at least ten of them, he estimated. He first walked along the edge of the spot where they had tethered their horses.

He saw mostly unshod Indian pony prints but spotted three sets of horseshoe hoof prints, horses taken from a settler or wagon train. He moved forward, scanning every mark, every indentation, every little depression of earth, grass, moss, and low brush. The earth, a combination of downy brome grass, soft topsoil and profuse weeds, and moss, gave its secrets to those who knew how to unravel them. The renegades carried rifles, he noted as he took in the thin, long depressions in the grass where they'd laid the guns. Small holes in the ground showed him that half of them also carried lances that had been thrust into the soil to stand upright and ready for instant use. The men had slept apart from each other, a practice that carried its own message. They were wily, he grunted, not without a grim appreciation. They practiced caution at all times. They'd not be targeted in a cluster.

Fargo knelt down and let his fingers sift through the grass still pressed down where the renegades had slept. As he moved from spot to spot little wisps of material came off on his fingers, linsey-woolsey caught on the edges of the grass, white man's wool. Blankets, he grunted, taken from their victims. Letting his fingers continue to explore the soil where

Excerpt from KIOWA COMMAND

each of the Indians had slept, he found bits and pieces of berries, prairie turnips, curcubita pepo and sunflower seeds, remains of their morning meal. But the meal leftovers were not at a camp meal spot. They were beside where each man had slept, and Fargo nodded at the message that gave him.

The renegades were so cautiously crafty they took their meals separately, unwilling to risk being caught eating together in a group or sleeping together. Fargo rose, his jaw tight. But he had a better picture of his quarry now. They were clever, acting together as a band, dependent on each other yet fully prepared to act individually, each man complete in himself with weapons and food. It was no doubt the key to their raids and attacks. They struck together and fled singly to regroup later at an agreed-upon spot. Fargo climbed onto the Ovaro and turned the horse southeast to find Lieutenant Elwood Siebert of Troop C, United States Cavalry, who had been following behind for the past three weeks. Orders of General Miles Stanford, of course.

Fargo let his thoughts go back to his last meeting with the general. Miles Stanford had sent three corporals to find him, obviously aware he'd be at the Brady ranch, since he'd brought Jack Brady's herd down from the Dakotas. The three soldiers escorted him to the general's headquarters at the bottom of Colorado Territory, a small but sturdy stockade fort from which the army patrolled all the way into Utah Territory. "You're looking fit as ever," Fargo told Miles

Excerpt from KIOWA COMMAND

with admiration. He had indeed never seen General Miles Stanford when he didn't look fit, a tall man with an imposing presence, prematurely silver hair in a young face. Miles was one of the better generals the army had sent into the untamed territories. "Of course, you didn't have your soldier boys bring me all the way down here because you miss me," Fargo said as he took the glass of bourbon offered him.

Miles Stanford chuckled as he raised his glass. "No, but it's damn good seeing you," he said. "It's been a good spell since we've worked together. You know I've always liked working with you, Fargo."

Fargo made a wry sound. "We've known each other too long for flattery. You've a problem, or you wouldn't have dragged me down here."

"You're growing too cynical," the general returned. "But you're right, of course. I've a problem, and it's called a rotten band of renegades. These are real bad actors, Fargo. They've been pulling off particularly brutal raids all over this territory. My patrols only find what they've left when they finish, which isn't much. I want to put a stop to them, and I need you to find them."

Fargo finished the bourbon as he spoke. "How many?"

"Wouldn't know. No survivors around to tell. But the best guess is anywhere from eight to twelve," the general said.

Fargo screwed his face up. "Twelve's a lot for a band of renegades," he said.

Excerpt from KIOWA COMMAND

"You're right, but I think they're maybe picking up more members each time. They've no pattern, no tribal roots, of course. But they keep crossing and crisscrossing the region. You could pick up a pattern and a trail. You're the only one I know who could. Extra pay for this one, old friend," Miles Stanford said and let himself look hopeful.

"What am I supposed to do if I find them? Take them on all by myself or come back here to report to you? They'll be on their way by the time I do that," Fargo said.

"I'm sending a patrol to follow along behind you," the general said.

"Far behind me," Fargo grunted.

"Far as you want," Miles said. "You find them, you go and get them, and they'll do the rest. I'm going to send Lieutenant Elwood Siebert to take the patrol. He's young, but he's got good training. He's out of the academy."

"Which means he's standard issue army shavetail," Fargo grunted. "Long on manuals, short on experience."

The general's lips tightened for a moment, but he made no protest, and Fargo allowed a grim snort to escape him. "I've told him about you. He's properly impressed," Miles said.

"Thanks, but what's that mean?" Fargo queried.

"He won't interfere with you. He'll take it slow as you want, stay back as far as you want, stop if you want him to stop. But he'll be there and ready when

Excerpt from KIOWA COMMAND

you need him. Of course, it'd be nice if you checked back with him once in a while."

"I haven't even agreed to do this, and you've got me checking back with him," Fargo protested.

"I expect you'll agree, old friend. I know you don't like renegades. Besides, I've something to sweeten the pot for you."

"Such as?" Fargo inquired.

"A real easy job at top dollar. By the time you get back, I expect a man named Burroughs to be here with two wagons of oriental silks he wants to get to the Missouri at St. Louis. He wrote ahead for an army scout. I can't give him one, of course, but I can give him you. It's a nice, clean job and, as I said, he'd offering top dollar. It's all yours. That sweet enough?" the general said, plainly pleased with his bargain.

"I guess so," Fargo conceded, and the general rose at once.

"Be right back. I want you to meet Lieutenant Siebert," he said, hurrying from the office to return moments later with a very young, tall, and ramrod-still junior officer in a sharply creased uniform. Fargo took in clear blue eyes, blondish hair cropped short, and an unlined face that tried to let earnestness take the place of maturity.

"Glad to meet you, sir," the lieutenant said with a crisp salute. "I look forward to riding with you."

Fargo groaned inwardly. "We won't be doing much riding together, Lieutenant," he said, then, softening his answer, "but I'll be depending on you when I'm

Excerpt from KIOWA COMMAND

ready." Elwood Siebert continued to look deadly earnest.

"You can count on me," he said and left the room with a snappy salute to the general.

"He'll do fine. He's a good young officer," the general said to Fargo when they were alone.

"Make sure he knows I'm calling the shots," Fargo grunted.

"Be ready to leave within the hour," Miles had said with a nod. That had been the start of it, Fargo murmured to himself as he clicked the pictures from his mind. He returned his eyes to the two ridges as he moved through a line of boxelder, away from the ridges and down into a tree-covered gulley. He continued to ride southeast and climbed out of the gully as his gaze moved along the horizon. He had told the lieutenant to ride slowly—"no dust plumes," he'd said—and now he had to live with that instruction. Slowly, he scanned each stretch of boxelder, hawthorn, and blackjack oak and silently swore as the sun moved higher into the sky. He found a high promontory that afforded a falcon's view of the countryside and was surveying in every direction when he caught the movement he searched for, branches being swayed in a straight line.

Putting the pinto into a gallop, he sent the horse downward, raced through trees and open spaces, and slowed only when he came in sight of the column of blue-clad riders. The lieutenant rode at the head of eighteen troopers and brought the column to a halt as

Excerpt from KIOWA COMMAND

Fargo rode up. "Found them," Fargo said, and Lieutenant Siebert's face filled with eager anticipation. "Couple of hours north," Fargo said as he swung the Ovaro around and began to lead the way. He slowed to a halt when they reached the second rise, and the lieutenant drew alongside him. "They're an hour or so past the next rise," Fargo said.

"That's all we need," Elwood Siebert said confidently.

"For what?" Fargo queried.

"To catch them on the run," the lieutenant said.

"You can't do that," Fargo said.

"Why not?" Siebert frowned.

"They'll hear you and see you. They'll take off," Fargo said.

"We'll be on them before they can get away. Our horses can outrun their short-legged ponies," Siebert said.

Fargo shook his head. "It won't work. You'll lose them all. These bastards won't act the way ordinary Indians would. An ordinary Indian band might decide to fight or run or both. But whatever they decided, they'd do as a unit. Not these. These are renegades, mister. They won't be fighting like ordinary Indians."

"You've a plan in mind, I take it," Siebert said with undisguised deprecation in his tone.

"Go a little farther, get a little closer on horseback, then dismount and close in on them on foot after they've settled down. Sneak up on them on foot and split your men into two groups," Fargo said.

Excerpt from KIOWA COMMAND

He saw the lieutenant's frown turn into chiding tolerance. "Mister Fargo, this is the United States cavalry. The cavalry doesn't attack on foot."

"It better this time," Fargo said grimly.

"Nonsense," Siebert said, and Fargo silently swore at the youthful arrogance in the officer's face. "Our horses can outrun those short-legged Indian ponies. We'll get them before they can scatter very far."

"Hell you will," Fargo snapped.

Siebert's face stayed infuriatingly smug. "I've made a specialty of pursuit-and-destroy operations. I know exactly how we'll get them. You are an outstanding trailsman, my dear man, but I'm afraid you're not a very good judge of military tactics."

"I'm a damn good judge of renegade tactics. You chase them your way and you'll get nothing except casualties," Fargo insisted.

The lieutenant's smile remained chiding. "You found them for us. We'll do the rest. You watch. I promise you results," he said.

"I'll make you a promise. I promise not to laugh," Fargo said and saw Siebert's lips tighten as he wheeled his horse to his troopers.

"Troop forward at the gallop," the lieutenant shouted and raced away.

"Shit," Fargo muttered, swerved the Ovaro as the troopers thundered past him. He rode the pinto at an angle, entered a stand of blackjack oak, and stayed in it as the lieutenant led his men up a passageway. Staying inside the trees, he stayed to the right of the

Excerpt from KIOWA COMMAND

passage and let the Ovaro go full out, finally passing the troopers as they had to slow when the passage narrowed and grew thick with foliage. He crested the rise, still going full out, confident of the Ovaro's powerful hindquarters, which gave him an agility the lieutenant's horses didn't possess. He drew away from the line of troopers, was a good hundred yards ahead of them when they crested the rise and found another open pathway. Riding hard, he stayed in the wooded terrain and glimpsed enough open land for the troopers to take. The renegades had taken the open passages, too, he was certain, and he estimated that almost an hour had passed when he glimpsed the small band of near-naked riders moving casually through a break of five-foot goosefoot.

Staying in the tree cover, he passed the Indians, slowing to a trot as he peered through the leaves. They were riding casually, and he glimpsed an Osage armband, a rawhide vest on another with very definitely Cheyenne beadwork, and a pouch carried by still another with a Kansa scroll design painted onto the leather. A tall renegade with long black hair rode slightly ahead of the others, his face long and lean with the heavy features of the Pawnee. Fargo edged still farther ahead and his eyes were on the renegades when he saw them suddenly stiffen and turn around on their ponies.

They had picked up the sound of the troopers. Fargo reined the pinto to a halt and leaped from the saddle, taking the big Henry from its saddle case. He

Excerpt from KIOWA COMMAND

held the rifle in one hand as he watched the Indians drop from their mounts and instantly separate, each man going into the tree cover beyond the goosefoot passage. His eyes were on the tall, lean one with the long black hair and the Pawnee face, and he saw the renegade lead his pony into the trees and then drop onto one knee, a rifle in his hands. He glimpsed another of the renegades some ten yards away, also melting into the trees. Glancing across the passage, he was able to catch a glimpse of two more of the renegades, apart from each other, as they sank into the tree cover. Fargo cursed silently. They were going to do exactly what he'd expected, exactly what they had practiced doing. They'd fire one volley, maybe two, cut down at least six or so troopers and then race away through the trees on both sides, each man moving separately from the others.

They'd let the troopers catch a glimpse of them, lure them into giving chase before they scattered like milkweed seeds. They'd disappear in all directions, each man a self-sufficient entity, needing neither to hunt for food nor to depend on someone else. Someplace, they had a prearranged place to meet. Fargo lifted the rifle to his shoulder. He couldn't let them all vanish untouched. He'd take down at least one, perhaps the leader. That could be enough to destroy the band. His finger rested on the rifle trigger as the lieutenant charged into view with his troops. One of the renegades rose into sight on the other side of the passage.

Excerpt from KIOWA COMMAND

The lieutenant reined his mount in at once, started to turn with his troops when the volley of shots exploded from both sides of the passage. Six of the troopers went down, and Fargo saw two others clutch their sides as they managed to stay on their horses. The renegade across the way dropped out of view as the rest of the troop milled in confusion and tried to take cover. Fargo's eyes moved to the lean-faced Indian as the redman leaped onto his pony and started to race away. He lay flat against his mount's back, but Fargo's sights were already following him. The big Henry erupted, a single shot, and the renegade fell sideways from his pony, one side of his head disappearing in a shower of red.

Fargo had already swung the rifle before the man hit the ground, catching sight of another of the renegades racing away. Once again the rifle barked, and the renegade toppled from his mount. Fargo whirled at a sound from his rear and was in time to see another of the Indians racing through the trees. He swung the Henry in a half circle, fired again, two shots this time, and saw the figure fall backward from the horse's back. Fargo returned his eyes to the other passage, where the troopers were trying to chase down the other renegades, riding wildly from side to side in the trees, some firing meaningless shots. The Indians had already disappeared, charging away through the trees, each figure alone, a will-o'-the-wisp flash glimpsed for but a brief moment. The troopers were still charging through the trees, in aim-

Excerpt from KIOWA COMMAND

less pursuit, and Fargo rose to his feet and walked to the Ovaro.

He led the pinto out of the trees by the reins and stopped where the lieutenant sat his horse, his eyes filled with shock. "It was all so fast," Elwood Siebert murmured, his voice hollow.

"You never got a chance to use those military tactics the manuals taught you," Fargo said. He peered at the lieutenant's suddenly older face. "It happens that way out here, son," he said, and Siebert's eyes stared back. "You grow up all of a sudden." The lieutenant swallowed hard as the other troopers began straggling back.

"They got away, every damn one of them," one of the soldiers said with bitterness coating his words.

"Three of them didn't," Fargo said. "You'll find them in the trees back there. One of them might have been their leader. If so, that could be the end of them."

"How'll we know?" Siebert asked.

"We won't," Fargo said. "Not for a while."

"How long would it take you to track down the rest of them?" the lieutenant asked.

"A month, maybe two. Too long. This mission's over. Go back and report," Fargo said.

"You're not coming?" Siebert asked.

"In a few days. I want a little time," Fargo said.

"To get over my not listening to you," Siebert said.

"That's part of it. To get over losing. I don't like losing," Fargo said.

Excerpt from KIOWA COMMAND

"I'll tell General Stanford it was my fault," the lieutenant said, a little stiffly.

"Never expected you wouldn't," Fargo said honestly. The younger man's nod said that he understood and was grateful for the trust. One of the troopers told the lieutenant they'd suffered four killed and four wounded. Fargo swung onto the Ovaro and rode away, feeling bitterness claw at him. It hadn't been his fault, but that didn't help any. That just let him avoid feeling guilty. Bitterness came with the knowing that things could turn wrong so quickly in this land. It was a feeling he knew only one way to drown, and he turned the horse north. A tiny cluster of buildings that had the effrontery to call itself a town lay but a day's ride into Colorado Territory. Ellie Smith lived there. Leastways she had two years ago. He expected she still did. Ellie had never been the roving kind, and he let memories quicken the pace as he rode.

It was afternoon the next day when he reached Ellie Smith's place, a little house and a small patch of land where she grew vegetables and baked biscuits and pies for the equally small travelers' inn nearby. She exploded with delight when she saw him ride to a halt and was hanging onto him in seconds. They talked of old times and old moments into the night, and when they lay naked together it was as if there had been no years in between. Ellie Smith had always been one of those women who carried ten to fifteen pounds extra and looked the better for it. Ellie

Excerpt from KIOWA COMMAND

was a creature of roundness, round face more pleasant than pretty, round shoulders, round breasts made for caressing, soft, round ass made for enjoying, not a single angular, sharp line to her. Ellie's personality matched her physical self, a clear case of the flesh and the spirit borrowing from each other.

Ellie was exactly what he needed, no pretense to her, no false coyness, just wonderful, enveloping warmth. The round breasts were magnificent pillows against his face, and he reveled in their cushioned warmth, in tasting of the full red-brown nipples that seemed to epitomize Ellie's frank womanliness. "Yes, yes, oh God, so long . . . so damn long," Ellie gasped as his hard-muscled body came against the round little belly. She thrust herself upward, moving the dark, fibrous-like triangle against his crotch, pressing, seeking, and then screaming as his own firm warmth slid into her. Memories flowed over Fargo, the past mingling with the present, all the enveloping passions echoing again, today made sweeter by yesterday.

He enjoyed Ellie through the night, as she enjoyed him, until they finally slept through the beginning of the new day. When she woke, he enjoyed watching her unself-conscious radiance as she stayed naked as she prepared breakfast. He stayed two more days and nights with Ellie, in which it seemed they both tried to encompass all of today and tomorrow, and finally he lay with her, exhausted but, in that special way of pure sensual communication, cleansed, the bitter-

Excerpt from KIOWA COMMAND

ness gone from him. "Don't wait another two years," Ellie said to him as he prepared to leave.

"I'll try not to," he told her. Ellie would hold to that, he knew, even as she realized it was no promise. He left then and, turning the Ovaro southeast, headed for Miles Stanford's stockade.

DESERT HAWKS
BY FRANK BURLESON

The year was 1846—and the great American Southwest was the prize in an epic conflict. The U.S. Army and the army of Mexico met in a battle that would shape the course of history, while the legendary Apache warrior chief Mangus Coloradas looked on, determined to defend his ancestral lands and age-old tribal traditions against either of the invaders or both. On this bloody battlefield young Lieutenant Nathanial Barrington faced his first great test of manhood ... as he began a career that would take him to the heart of the conflict sweeping over the West from Texas to New Mexico ... and plunge him into passion that would force him to choose between two very different frontier beauties. This enthralling first novel of *The Apache Wars* trilogy captures the drama and real history of a struggle in which no side wanted to surrender ... in a series alive with all the excitement, adventure of brave men and women—white and Native American—who decided the future of America.

from **SIGNET**

Buy them at your local bookstore or use this convenient coupon for ordering.

PENGUIN USA
P.O. Box 999 — Dept. #17109
Bergenfield, New Jersey 07621

Please send me the books I have checked above.
I am enclosing $_____ (please add $2.00 to cover postage and handling). Send check or money order (no cash or C.O.D.'s) or charge by Mastercard or VISA (with a $15.00 minimum). Prices and numbers are subject to change without notice.

Card #_____ Exp. Date _____
Signature_____
Name_____
Address_____
City _____ State _____ Zip Code _____

For faster service when ordering by credit card call **1-800-253-6476**

Allow a minimum of 4-6 weeks for delivery. This offer is subject to change without notice.

WAR EAGLES
BY FRANK BURLESON

In the North, a lanky lawyer named Abraham Lincoln was recovering from a brutal political setback. In the South, eloquent U.S. Senator Jefferson Davis was risking all in a race for governor of his native Mississippi. And far to the Southwest, the future of the frontier was being decided as the U.S. Army, under Colonel Bull Moose Sumner, faced the growing alliance of Native Americans led by the great Mangus Colorados and determined to defend their ancestral lands. For First Lieutenant Nathanial Barrington it was his first test as a professional soldier following orders he distrusted in an undeclared war without conscience or quarter—and his test as a man when he met the Apache woman warrior Jocita in a night lit by passion that would yield to a day of dark decision ...

from SIGNET

Buy them at your local bookstore or use this convenient coupon for ordering.

PENGUIN USA
P.O. Box 999 — Dept. #17109
Bergenfield, New Jersey 07621

Please send me the books I have checked above.
I am enclosing $_____ (please add $2.00 to cover postage and handling). Send check or money order (no cash or C.O.D.'s) or charge by Mastercard or VISA (with a $15.00 minimum). Prices and numbers are subject to change without notice.

Card #_____ Exp. Date _____
Signature_____
Name_____
Address_____
City _____ State _____ Zip Code _____

For faster service when ordering by credit card call **1-800-253-6476**

Allow a minimum of 4-6 weeks for delivery. This offer is subject to change without notice.

THE DAWN OF FURY
BY RALPH COMPTON

Nathan Stone had experienced the horror of Civil War battlefields. But the worst lay ahead. When he returned to Virginia, to the ruins of what had been his home, his father had been butchered and his mother and sister stripped, ravished, and slain. The seven renegades who had done it had ridden away into the West. Half-starved and afoot, Nathan Stone took their trail. Nathan Stone's deadly oath—blood for blood—would cost him seven long years, as he rode the lawless trails of an untamed frontier. His skill with a Colt would match him equally with the likes of the James and Youngers, Wild Bill Hickok, John Wesley Hardin, and Ben Thompson. Nathan Stone became the greatest gunfighter of them all, shooting his way along the most relentless vengeance trail a man ever rode to the savage end ... and this is how it all began.

from **SIGNET**

Buy them at your local bookstore or use this convenient coupon for ordering.

PENGUIN USA
P.O. Box 999 — Dept. #17109
Bergenfield, New Jersey 07621

Please send me the books I have checked above.
I am enclosing $_____ (please add $2.00 to cover postage and handling). Send check or money order (no cash or C.O.D.'s) or charge by Mastercard or VISA (with a $15.00 minimum). Prices and numbers are subject to change without notice.

Card #_____ Exp. Date _____
Signature_____
Name_____
Address_____
City _____ State _____ Zip Code _____

For faster service when ordering by credit card call **1-800-253-6476**

Allow a minimum of 4-6 weeks for delivery. This offer is subject to change without notice.

THE BORDER CAPTAINS
BY JASON MANNING

The fledgling United States has survived the Revolutionary War. And with the turn of the new century, settlers are poised to continue their westward thrust through the dark and bloody killing grounds of Kentucky. But in their path stands the British military's might, and an even more menacing and worthy foe—the brilliant, brave and legendary Native American chief Tecumseh. The War of 1812 is about to begin. And in the hands of such American heroes as "Mad" Anthony Wayne, William Henry Harrison, Henry Clay, and Daniel Boone . . . with the trigger fingers of a buckskin-clad army . . . and in the courage, daring and determination of frontiersman Nathaniel "Flintlock" Jones . . . history is to be made, a wilderness to be won, and a spellbinding saga of the American past is to be brought to pulse-pounding, unforgettable life . . .

The Border Captains is the second epic historical novel of the Flintlock trilogy, written by the acclaimed author of the *High Country* frontier novels.

from SIGNET

Buy them at your local bookstore or use this convenient coupon for ordering.

PENGUIN USA
P.O. Box 999 — Dept. #17109
Bergenfield, New Jersey 07621

Please send me the books I have checked above.
I am enclosing $_____ (please add $2.00 to cover postage and handling). Send check or money order (no cash or C.O.D.'s) or charge by Mastercard or VISA (with a $15.00 minimum). Prices and numbers are subject to change without notice.

Card #_____ Exp. Date _____
Signature_____
Name_____
Address_____
City _____ State _____ Zip Code _____

For faster service when ordering by credit card call **1-800-253-6476**

Allow a minimum of 4-6 weeks for delivery. This offer is subject to change without notice.

GONE TO TEXAS
BY JASON MANNING

In 1839, when President Andrew Jackson decides it is time for Texas to gain its independence from Mexico, he calls upon Flintlock Jones and his grandson Christopher Groves. The pair can't wait to get into the action but get more than they bargained for when kidnappers, river pirates, cutthroats, and bounty hunters lie in wait for them on a blood-soaked trail from Kentucky to hostile Texas territory. It is grizzled, old Flintlock's most dangerous mission—as revolutionaries and their enemies fight each other with a passion that blazes hotter than the Texas sun.

Gone to Texas is the gripping conclusion to the epic Flintlock trilogy, written by the acclaimed author of the *High Country* frontier novels.

from SIGNET

Buy them at your local bookstore or use this convenient coupon for ordering.

PENGUIN USA
P.O. Box 999 — Dept. #17109
Bergenfield, New Jersey 07621

Please send me the books I have checked above.
I am enclosing $_____ (please add $2.00 to cover postage and handling). Send check or money order (no cash or C.O.D.'s) or charge by Mastercard or VISA (with a $15.00 minimum). Prices and numbers are subject to change without notice.

Card #_____ Exp. Date _____
Signature_____
Name_____
Address_____
City _____ State _____ Zip Code _____

For faster service when ordering by credit card call **1-800-253-6476**

Allow a minimum of 4-6 weeks for delivery. This offer is subject to change without notice.